THE BAY OF STRANGERS

Lillian Beckwith was born in Ellesmere Port, Cheshire, where her father owned a grocery business thus providing the background for her book *About My Father's Business*.

Shortly before the last war she went to live in the Hebrides where she stayed for nearly twenty years, living and working on her own croft. Her experiences there resulted in her Hebridean books *The Hills is Lonely, The Sea for Breakfast* etc.

In addition she has written novels and short stories. Her hobbies are cooking and entertaining, beachcombing and travelling.

THE BAY
OF STRANGERS

Lillian Beckwith

ARROW BOOKS

For 'Tommy' (Dorothy Tomlinson)
without whose encouragement I would have been
a 'one book' writer.

Arrow Books Limited
62–65 Chandos Place, London WC2N 4NW

An imprint of Century Hutchinson Limited

London Melbourne Sydney Auckland
Johannesburg and agencies throughout
the world

First published in Great Britain by Century 1988
Arrow edition 1989

Printed and bound in Great Britain by
Anchor Press Limited, Tiptree, Essex

ISBN 0 09 959980 5

Contents

THE BAY OF STRANGERS

Glossary		Approximate pronunciation
cailleach	old woman	kyle-yak
ceilidh	an impromptu gathering for chat or entertainment	cayley
crowdie	a soft curd cheese	(as spelled)
gey	very	gay
oidhche mhath	goodnight!	oi-she-va
sgurr	a skerry or conical outcrop of rock	(as spelled)
strupak	a cup of tea and a bite to eat	strupak
stirk	a yearling heifer or bullock	(as spelled)
girdle	griddle	(as spelled)
lochan	a small inland loch	lockan
sneck	a latch	
Cruelty	SSPCA	
first footer	the first person to enter a house in the New Year	

1

The Bay of Strangers

Neil Cameron was forty years old when he decided the time had come for him to 'speak for' Catriona McRae.

The intention to do so had begun to take shape in his mind some three years previously but since Catriona had been then only ten years of age he knew he must wait some little time before he could make his approach to her mother. Meantime he had watched Catriona develop from a frolic-some youngster into a responsible young girl sturdy enough to help her widowed mother with the work of the croft and able and willing enough to row a boat and bring home a catch of fish. Neil, continuing to assess her merits, was confident she would make a good wife for him when the time came for her to marry. So it was that on the eve of Catriona's thirteenth birthday, which happened to be the night before Halloween, Neil was in his lamplit bedroom preparing himself for his delicate and important mission.

The room was small and despite the minimal amount of home-built furniture would have been cramped for a man only half Neil's stature. Even sitting on the bed to dress himself he had to be careful of his movements for fear of knocking over the oil lamp which stood on the chest between the bed and the window. He reached for a clean shirt and pulling it over his head struggled to tuck the tail into the trousers of his dark Sabbath suit which though old in years, was still relatively new due to lack of wear. Bending forward he eased his stockinged feet into seldom worn shoes, grimacing slightly at the restraint which even well-fitting shoes imposed on feet that were more accustomed to the roominess of gumboots. He then put on his knitted tie, tying it without the aid of a mirror since the room boasted no such luxury, and finally he eased himself into his jacket which the years had tightened over his muscular arms and shoulders. He brushed his hair and passed the roughened palms of his hands over his suit to remove the fragments of down and tiny feathers which inevitably drifted through to his room and attached themselves to his clothes whenever his mother plucked a chicken in the kitchen. Satisfied, he picked up the lamp and, bending his head so as to avoid the low door frame, he opened the door into the kitchen.

His mother was standing by the table with her hands in a bowl of soapy water, washing the dishes they had used for their evening meal. Behind her the peat fire, made up in readiness for the anticipated respite from the day's work, glowed its invitation. His mother glanced up at him as he entered and out of the corner of his eye he noted the fleeting expression of surprise that crossed her face.

'You're away visiting?' Her tone was deliberately un-inquisitive.

'Aye so,' Neil affirmed, suspecting she had instantly divined his purpose. It had irritated him when he was younger that his mother had seemed able to sense his most secret thoughts, and there had been times when he had come to believe she must be gifted with the 'second sight', but now he accepted that it was no unusual gift she possessed save that of being highly perceptive. Careful as he had been to betray no sign of his choice of future wife having fallen on Catriona, he thought it likely that some preoccupied glance or unguarded action of his had been sufficient to reveal to her his intention.

Opening the outside door he stood there, the tall bulk of him filling the doorway. 'I've seen to the calves and closed up the hens,' he told her before she could put the question to him. 'And there's plenty of peats beside the door here so you'll not be needing to go out of the house yourself tonight, cailleach.'

The old woman straightened her bent back as well as she could and wiped her wet hands on her apron. 'Aye,' she acknowledged expressionlessly. Her glance rested on his broad back, but fearing he might turn suddenly and detect the glow of pride she had in him, she shifted her gaze to the square of darkness that was the uncurtained window. 'It's a grand night in the Bay of Strangers,' she observed, and when he did not answer she went on, 'I was after lifting a few peats into the pail a wee whiley since and there was the moon looking like a great golden egg in the cup of the hills and it looking down into the bay as if it was fearing it might take a tumble into it, just.'

Neil's lips moved fractionally. Taciturn as he was by nature it did not make him any the less patient with his mother's garrulousness, which tended to flow more abundantly when she was a little disturbed, as he guessed she was now.

'It's a grand night indeed,' he agreed, smiling into the darkness. His mother's predilection for speaking of the bay as if she were reading its name from a map rarely failed to amuse him. To Neil and to the other islanders the bay was simply 'the bay'. The reason it had at some time been characterized as the Bay of Strangers scarcely interested them since it belonged to an age before they or their forebears had set foot on the island and consequently no folklore was attached to it. For a while Neil lingered as if contemplating the darkness. His mother watched him covertly, gloating in the stalwart son she had reared.

'I'll be away then,' he called over his shoulder, and going out into the night closed the door behind him.

After she had dried and replaced the dishes on the dresser the old woman sat down on the high-backed wooden chair strategically placed beside the fire and within easy reach of the kettle and the peat box. It was her own special chair, fashioned for her by her husband from prized pieces of driftwood and then presented to her on the day they were married. Since that day it had stood in the same position as it stood now and where it would continue to stand so long as she was alive. Draped over the back of the chair was a worn woollen pullover of Neil's, half unpicked, and this she took on to her lap, resuming the unpicking while she stared meditatively into the fireglow and allowed a smile of contentment to soften the mouth that had been so tightened by adversity. As soon as Neil had appeared, dressed, in the kitchen she had indeed guessed where he was bound for and she had no doubt as to the purpose of his errand.

It was good, she mused, that Neil was thinking of taking a wife, for surely the time was coming when she herself would no longer be able to cope with much of the outdoor work of the croft. Though recognizing the inevitable she saw no urgent need to bring another woman into the household. She was proud to consider herself still capable of carrying on with those tasks which were traditionally a woman's work, but on the other hand there was no denying that increasing age sometimes pressed hard on her shoulders and shortened her breath, giving her cause to allow herself to think how comforting it would be to be rid of the dread of going out on to the moors in all weathers to see to the cattle; of having to wrestle with unruly calves; of being tortured by her aching back as she strove to keep up with the harvesting. For sixty years, ever since she had been old enough to carry home a pail of milk from the hill, she had been steeped in work. Now she could look forward to the day when she could sit here in her chair beside the fire while a young woman took over the tasks of carrying water from the well; of lifting the heavy pans from the fire and of feeding the poultry when the path to their shed was treacherous with ice. Yes, her thoughts assured her, she would truly welcome Catriona into her home even if it would lead to a lessening of her own authority there, and in the years between now and the chosen time for the marriage – and there would be no undue haste, of that the old woman was certain – Catriona would have plenty of opportunity to prepare herself to be Neil's wife.

There had been times since Neil had reached manhood when the old woman had feared his getting himself married. Feared that following one of his annual trips to Glasgow where he went to look at boatyards and keep in touch with fishmarkets he might return with a city wife who would be totally unfitted for island life. She had judged it an unlikely possibility but, she had reminded herself, was not Neil a man? And a fine, handsome man who could easily cause a young woman's heart to flutter. And who would know better than herself that men, even the best of men, could behave foolishly enough to make their womenfolk hold up their hands in horror? Her relief when she had seen that Neil's choice had settled on Catriona had been like the releasing of a too-tight creel rope across her breast. He had never spoken to her of his resolve. He had not needed to since even before he himself had become fully aware of his aspiration to some day marry Catriona, his mother, in her shrewd, far-seeing way, had worked it out for herself. Catriona might have been only a young lassie but it had not escaped the old woman's notice that Neil, who had always been a favourite with the children of the island, had become increasingly offhand in his behaviour towards the girl. The clue had thus presented itself. It was a characteristic she had observed in him from his earliest childhood – the more he cared for something the harder he had always tried to conceal his feelings.

There was no question in the old woman's mind but that Neil's bespeaking of Catriona would be welcomed by both the girl and her mother. What lassie would not be delighted to be chosen by such a man as Neil? What widow-woman would not welcome such fine expectations for her daughter? Wasn't he the most respected of men? she questioned herself . . . Was he not tall and strong, fearless and hard working? Was his croft not the best tended? And was there any man who could match his skill at fishing? Didn't the lobsters he caught in his creels bring him good money from London? Good enough for him to have an account at a bank on the mainland. Once, she recalled, when she had managed to steal a peep at his bank book the figures she had seen there had made her gasp with astonishment. Oh yes, Neil would be a great catch for any woman. And young as she was Catriona would be wise enough to know she would be getting the very best of husbands. The old woman nodded ruminatively at the flames. And my! she told herself, would not Catriona be the proud one when she got to know of her good fortune? Surely it was a rare enough thing for a girl to be spoken for when she was no more than thirteen years old?

5

* * *

Preoccupied with his intention Neil strode unhurriedly along the stony path which skirted the broad semi-circle of the bay to terminate as it neared a spread of croft houses on the opposite shore. Against the background of the moor the cottages loomed pearly white, their lamplit windows dimmed into insignificance by the effulgent moonlight. The bay was whisper quiet, the moon-sheened ripples licking demurely at the shingle. Neil's own footsteps crunching on the path were the only other sounds of the night.

Ordinarily he would have rowed across the bay rather than walk all the way round, but since one would not think of bespeaking a future wife while wearing one's working clothes and since one would not don one's Sabbath suit and shoes only to risk their being spoiled by sitting in a workaday and consequently fish-offal-splashed and tar-sticky dinghy, he had chosen to walk. When he reached the cottage where Catriona lived with her mother and younger brother he lifted the sneck of the door and pushed it open, at the same time announcing himself by calling out a greeting.

In response Catriona's mother, Lexy, warmly enjoined him to 'Come away in!' Lexy was sitting beside the fire knitting a complicated pattern of a jersey and as Neil appeared in the doorway of the kitchen she gave him a broad smile of welcome. 'Why, it's yourself, Neil,' she exclaimed and immediately began to feel a little flustered. She herself had had an intuitive suspicion that Neil might be looking for a wife and that his choice might have fallen on her daughter. For some months the possibility of a visit from him had been lurking at the back of her mind and now seeing him dressed in his Sabbath clothes she had no doubt as to the reason for his visit. She rose quickly from her chair and, swinging the kettle over the fire, stirred the peats under it so as to hurry it to the boil. It was unthinkable for her not to offer Neil a strupak; equally unthinkable for him to refuse it. He sat down on the bench and, noticing the slight nervousness in her manner, he knew instantly that only the timing of his visit had come as a surprise to her.

'You're on your own?' he remarked as she put a plate of scones before him. The degree of surprise in his voice was entirely assumed. He had overheard the schoolchildren arranging to go over to the shepherd's house that evening and he had been certain Catriona and her brother would not have stayed behind.

'I am so,' Lexy replied. 'Catriona and Alistair are away with all the other young rascals to Duncan's to beg fleece for their Halloween masks,' she confirmed.

It was as Neil had planned. He had not wished Catriona to be present when he first broached the subject to her mother.

'Did you have good fishing today?' Lexy probed, busily buttering a scone for him.

'No bad,' he acknowledged.

'I'm after hearing they're paying good prices for lobsters,' she said, modulating her voice so it would not sound inquisitive.

'Not as high as you would expect,' Neil said guardedly. 'Lobsters are gey scarce just now and they should be bringing top prices.'

'That's true enough,' she agreed with a rueful sigh. 'But I daresay Londoners think lobsters are as easy caught as buses in a city street.' She rooted under the recess bed and produced a tin of shop shortbread. Opening it, she set it on the table in front of Neil. He ignored it. 'Do you not like shortbread then, Neil?' she demanded.

'Well enough, but not when I can choose your own baked scones,' he flattered her, and helped himself to another one. He stirred sugar into his tea and she thought he drank it with unaccustomed sedateness.

Lexy sat down and took up her knitting and they continued to talk with apparent ease, yet each knew the other was slowly and skilfully directing the conversation towards the subject that hovered between them.

'Are you thinking of sending any of your beasts to the cattle sale next month?' Neil asked with only moderate interest.

'I'm thinking maybe I'll send the two stirks,' she admitted. 'For all the price they're making these days I'm not likely to profit by keeping them until the spring.'

'I believe you'd be wise to sell them,' he allowed. 'If the winter's a bad one they'll lose condition fairly quickly.' He politely pushed his empty cup towards her and while she was refilling it he said, 'The cailleach's wanting me to get rid of some of my own beasts. She reckons they're getting too much for her to manage when I'm away on the hill or out fishing.' His voice took on a slightly jesting note as if he were seeking confirmation that his mother was indeed getting too old to cope. 'Ach, but I don't know whether to believe her,' he added.

Lexy, knowing him as a man who was hard on himself yet tender with any sign of weakness or frailty in others, knew how to follow his lead. 'Your mother does well for her age,' she told him. 'But right enough folks are saying now and then that she's not so strong as she used to be.' She handed him a second cup of tea, poured one for herself and set the pot back on the hob. 'Surely the time will come when you'll need to be thinking of getting someone younger about the place.' She could feel the tension mounting between them.

'Aye so,' Neil concurred.

She managed to get a teasing note into her voice. 'A wife maybe?' she suggested.

For Neil the moment had come. 'I've been thinking for a whiley now that in a few years' time your own Catriona will be making a good wife for a man,' he propounded, eyeing her steadily.

Without looking up from her knitting Lexy inclined her head in gracious acknowledgement. 'Indeed I'm sure that's true enough.' Her needles clicked more rapidly before she spoke again. 'And would you have in mind such a man, Neil?'

'I would so,' he said.

She could feel his eyes on her but she would not look up to meet them. 'But you'll not be wishing to say who it might be, is that it, Neil?' she fenced delicately.

'It is myself,' Neil admitted. Lexy looked up and there

was an interchange of glances that lasted a few seconds. The flushed patches which touched his cheekbones belied the air of imperturbability he was at pains to assume. 'Would you say Catriona might come to thinking that way herself when she's older?'

'She is gey young yet to be thinking that way at all,' Lexy said. 'Though she is older than her years in her sense,' she added. The thought flicked through her mind that he was nearer her own age than Catriona's.

'But you would do nothing to dissuade her?'

'When the time comes for her to marry she will not find herself a better husband,' Lexy granted. When the time came: she recalled her own marriage at the age of thirty-four to a man twenty-three years her senior. He had been a good man and theirs had been a good marriage. In, say, five years' time Catriona would be eighteen and of marriageable age. Neil would be forty-five . . . The disparity in their ages would not be too great for Neil and Catriona to make a good marriage.

'It is proud I would be to make Catriona my wife,' Neil assured her earnestly.

She looked up at him and her mouth curved itself into an approving smile. 'Catriona will be a proud lassie when she hears of it and I a proud mother,' she declared.

They shook hands. She produced a bottle of whisky and two glasses from the dresser cupboard and they sealed their pledge in the time-honoured way.

When Neil rose to go he said, 'It is best that I myself do not speak to Catriona of this. Not until she is older and it is nearer the time. But you will tell her yourself what we have been speaking of tonight?'

'I will tell her the day after Halloween,' she promised. 'Until then her mind will be too full of mischief to take in anything else.'

Catriona was dazed by the excitement of Neil's proposal. It was breathtaking! It was a wonderful, wonderful thing to have happened! To think that she Catriona McRae now had the distinction of having been spoken for when she was only

9

just thirteen years old. Moreover she had been spoken for by the man everyone agreed was the most handsome, the most respected, the most eligible man on the island! What other girl had ever been able to boast of being paid such a compliment? For days she felt almost dizzy with delight. She had so much to look forward to. She would soon learn to love Neil as a wife should love a prospective husband. And then when she reached the age of eighteen or thereabouts he would claim her and she would share his home, his croft and his prosperity. She would share his bed and she would bear his children. What happiness they would be able to look forward to!

Much to her disappointment her mother made her promise to continue to treat Neil as she and all the children had always treated him. Neither by action nor expression must she reveal any sign of their betrothment. Until Neil had decided the time had come to publicly proclaim his intention she must keep the secret to herself. Dismayed by the stipulation, Catriona was too well conditioned to obedience to have attempted to defy it. She contented herself by piously thanking her God for having so blest her, and praying that the intervening years would pass quickly.

Five years went by and during that time Neil's attitude to Catriona had remained uncompromising. He had made no attempt to see her alone and the recognition of their commitment to each other was confined to an occasional proprietorial glance from Neil reciprocated by a coy and, at times, daringly coquettish glance from the mischievous Catriona. Then, one evening shortly before her eighteenth birthday, Neil, once more dressed in his Sabbath suit, walked the shingle path in the direction of Catriona's home.

Catriona was expecting him. Indeed she had been eagerly anticipating his visit ever since her seventeenth birthday, by which time she had considered herself quite old enough to marry. Following the usual polite exchange of comment and inquiries and the inevitable cup of tea, Neil turned his attention to her mother.

'I will be away to Glasgow very soon,' he announced.

10

'Is that so?' murmured Lexy. 'And will you be staying long?'

'For a week just,' he said. He shot a glance at Catriona who was intent on darning one of her brother's stockings. 'I was thinking maybe Catriona would care to come along with me, if she has a mind that way.'

Catriona felt her heart begin to pound with excitement. She and Neil could not go anywhere together unless they were married, surely? And now he was saying he was going 'very soon'. And to Glasgow! She had never been further than the tiny village on the mainland and a trip to Glasgow had been a long-cherished dream. Reminding herself of her mother's injunction to assume an air of aloofness rather than eagerness, she shook her long dark hair over her face to hide her burning cheeks.

'Well, Catriona? What have you to say to Neil?' Her mother was looking at her fixedly, compelling her to make her own answer.

Catriona's heart was racing, so it was a moment before she could speak. 'I would dearly like to go to Glasgow with Neil,' she said, and lifting her head managed to give him a prim smile.

Neil rose, his grim mouth relaxed a little. 'Do you wish I should speak to the minister about us then, Catriona?'

Catriona looked anxiously at her mother, who was regarding her with an expression of gentle encouragement. As her lips framed the words of her reply Catriona's stomach tautened with gladness. 'You will be right to do that, Neil,' she said, and glancing up at him caught the glint of happiness in his eyes. Looking at Lexy, Neil received her nod of confirmation of the arrangement.

When the announcement of the forthcoming wedding was made no one questioned the disparity in the age between the prospective bride and groom since by island reckoning Catriona was now a fully mature and sensible young woman while Neil, at forty-five, was regarded as being still a young man. It was natural that an active and pretty young woman should wish to marry a man with so much to commend him as Neil. It was just as natural for

11

such a man to want a strong young wife who had plenty of childbearing years ahead of her.

Two weeks later they were married in the little church and everyone in the island came to the wedding: the young and the aged; the lusty and the infirm; and for three days afterwards there was such a feasting and drinking that every house opened its doors to the revelry, there being no one house large enough to hold all the guests. There was much praise of Neil's liberality in providing such abundance and when at last the newly married couple boarded Tearlach's boat which was to take them to the mainland where they would catch the train for Glasgow the jetty was thronged with high-spirited neighbours. Catriona, proud of the gold ring which custom decreed she should wear only on the Sabbath, could recall no time in her life when she had been so gloriously happy.

After a week's stay with relatives in Glasgow – no one spoke of it as being a honeymoon since honeymoons had never been part of the marriage ritual – they returned to the island, to their home and to the querulousness of Neil's mother. Catriona, conditioned to a matriarchal environment and knowing that the old woman's bouts of crotchetiness were merely her way of asserting her intention of remaining mistress of the house for as long as she was able, accepted her inferior position with equanimity. After all, she reasoned, there was plenty of croft work to keep her occupied and when their bairns began to come along, as they surely would, she would be glad to have the old woman's help with looking after them. Catriona gloried in her new status.

A year went by and towards the end of it she was conscious of a shadow creeping over her happiness. Brought up in a community which regarded the begetting of children as the first joy of marriage, she had confidently expected that by now she would have borne Neil a child or at least have been pregnant, but despite frequent and ever more fervent prayers she had so far detected not the slightest sign of pregnancy. She longed to have a child to nurse, longed to make Neil a father. As the months went by the fear that she might be unable to conceive began to nag at her.

Meantime, now that she had taken over much of the outside work, Neil had felt able to buy in more cattle and sheep; to make more lobster creels and to stay out fishing for longer periods than hitherto. As a result they had prospered to the extent that Neil had suggested they enlarge the cottage by adding a couple of extra rooms. Catriona, reacting eagerly to his suggestion, hugged to herself the reason she surmised was behind it.

'I'm thinking you must be meaning to take in tourists,' Neil's mother had probed when building had begun.

'Maybe so,' Catriona had responded lightly. Certainly the extra rooms would be useful for accommodating the occasional tourists should they ever wish to do so, but privately she scoffed at the idea of their being used for that purpose.

A second year passed. And then a third and when Catriona still showed no sign of bearing a child the good-natured chaffing and bawdy innuendo to which all newly married couples were subjected by the neighbours had run its course. Now all she was conscious of were looks of puzzled scrutiny or silent pity. Shamed by her failure to conceive, she became over-sensitive, imagining she saw despair in Neil's attitude and censure in her mother-in-law's occasional comment.

Her own mother had taxed her outright. 'Why no bairns yet, Catriona?' She had sounded disapproving as if she suspected her daughter was wilfully delaying conception, but seeing the dumb bleakness of Catriona's expression her tone had changed immediately to compassion. 'Ach, there's plenty of time yet, lassie. Plenty of time,' she had consoled her daughter, but Catriona knew that she too was puzzled.

When the time came for Neil's next trip to Glasgow Catriona, much to his surprise, stated her intention of remaining at home. When he questioned her she gave as her reason that his mother was now too frail to be left alone to cope with even the minimal amount of croft work which would require attention during their absence. He argued and coaxed, reminding her of how much she had always looked forward to the annual trip, but she became so testy and tight-lipped he gave up, and if he ever suspected that her true reason for not accompanying him was that she had come to dread the raised eyebrows and the flippant but still hurtful insinuations of the numerous relatives which convention demanded they must visit, he did not voice his suspicions.

While Neil was absent in Glasgow Catriona carried on with the necessary croft work. The spring work had been completed: the peats cut and stacked, the potatoes planted and the corn sown, so apart from regularly attending to the animals she had only to bring home the twice daily creel full of peats. Then, if the weather was sufficiently calm and if she felt so inclined, she could indulge in her favourite pastime which was to drag the small dinghy down to the water and row out into the bay for the purpose of catching a fry of fish for their evening meal.

She was thus indulging herself in the late evening of what had been a day full of sunshine when she heard the distant throb of an engine, and screening her eyes from the still-bright sun she perceived a small yacht rounding the spur of rock which like a thin black finger pointed to the entrance to the bay. She was a little surprised. In high summer it was not too unusual for small boats to put into the bay seeking a safe anchorage for the night but the tourist season had not yet begun and though the weather was mild, even warm, it was still too early in the year to be confident that the savagery of a winter gale might not suddenly transform the sheltered waters of the bay into a churning hazard of white breakers. With a mixture of curiosity and disapproval she watched the boat making steadily towards the shore. She heard the engine being throttled down as the boat circled investigatively and then it was revved up again and she saw that the boat was making straight towards her. As it approached the engine was cut to a slow pulsing. Catriona waited composedly for the yacht to draw alongside.

'I say!' a young man called from the cockpit. 'D'you happen to know a good place to moor for the night?' He stepped up on to the deck.

She had been anticipating his question since it was one she had been asked many times before, but the easy answer she had been ready to give was checked by a gasp of consternation. Never in her life had she been confronted by a male figure so naked and so close.

She had been married to Neil for three years but Neil always turned down the lamp before he started to undress, and even then he never took off his shirt. Though her hands knew his body she had never seen him nearly so naked as the young man who was now standing so unashamedly before her, his scanty swimming trunks seeming to emphasize rather than conceal his maleness. The day's sun had fired her cheeks but now she was aware of a deeper, almost painful burning. Her throat grew parched. Her eyes slid away from him as he crouched to lean over the bow and hold on to the gunwale of the dinghy.

She steadied her voice. 'How much do you draw?' she asked, resolutely looking him straight in the eye because it seemed the safest place for her to fix her attention. He told her. It was a relief to turn and point towards the shore. 'See the old ruin there the other side of the burn?' He looked and nodded. 'You'll take a straight line out from that until you see the wee house there in the cove. There's a good two fathoms there.' She took up her oars again as an indication that she wished to resume rowing but instead of returning to the cockpit he kept his hold of the gunwale.

'Good fishing?' he asked.

'Not bad,' she allowed.

'What's the swimming like here?' he pursued.

Catriona shrugged. 'Not to my liking,' she told him. She had no wish to prolong the encounter and as a hint to him she began pushing with an oar against the yacht's side. He released his hold and jumped back into the cockpit.

'Good luck with the fishing,' he called. She managed a stiff smile of acknowledgement and then looked away quickly, disallowing the approval that was plain in his eyes.

When she had caught a good fry of fish she rowed back to the shore and as she was busy gutting and cleaning her catch at the water's edge she heard the yacht's dinghy being lowered into the water. Seconds later it was being rowed towards her and on reaching the shallow water the young man leapt out and pulled the dinghy a little way up the shingle. Catriona felt her cheeks begin to burn again as he approached. He had covered his nakedness with a thin shirt but as he paused beside her she was hotly aware that her rebellious inner eye was discarding the garment, compelling her to see again the bare, sun-tanned flesh; the firm muscles; the track of thick fair hair that travelled from above his chest to below his trunks.

'Hello again!' he greeted her. Without looking at him she murmured a shy acknowledgement. 'Is there somewhere I can buy milk and eggs?' he inquired. She noticed he was carrying a can and an egg box.

Conscious of his boldly admiring gaze, Catriona retaliated by affecting a tart irritability. 'Go up to the cottage there and tell the old woman what you want and that I sent you,' she directed, gesturing towards her mother-in-law's house. She did not tell him that the old woman, like all the other neighbours, would not only have watched the yacht coming into the bay but would have observed his every movement since then. Head bent, she continued to gut the fish but the young man made no move to go.

'They look good,' he commented. 'Would you consider letting me buy a couple from you for my supper?'

'You are welcome to take a couple of fish,' she offered coolly, and flicked a couple over the shingle to land at his feet.

'Gosh!' he exclaimed. 'That's wonderful. I shall certainly enjoy those. But, look, are you sure I can't . . .?' She did not speak but her manner disdained his intended offer. He crouched down and picked up the fish and continued to crouch, watching her until she had finished the gutting.

'What now?' he asked as she rose.

'I shall be taking them back to the house,' she replied. 'You'd best follow me if you're wanting milk and eggs.'

He tried to draw her into conversation as they walked together but though Catriona would have dearly liked to know the purpose of his visit at such a time of year she was

16

too tongue-tied to respond with anything but shy, mono-syllabic answers to his questions and comments.

The old woman was standing in the doorway of the cottage. Catriona went past her into the kitchen. 'He's wanting milk and eggs,' she said. 'You'll get them for him while I go and see to the hens.'

'Well, indeed but it's welcome you are to the Bay of Strangers on this beautiful evening,' the old woman greeted the young man. 'Come away in now while I get you what you're wanting.' She led the way inside and bade him sit down.

'The Bay of Strangers?' the young man repeated. 'Now that does sound interesting. Surely there must be a story to account for it having a name like that?'

Catriona interrupted with unaccustomed curtness. 'The young man is wanting eggs and milk and I daresay he will be wishing to get back to his boat so don't be keeping him back with your talk, cailleach!' She put the fish in the larder then slipped away, mumuring that it was time to close up the hens. She purposely lingered over the task, hoping the young man would be back at his boat when she returned to the house but she was dismayed to see his dinghy still on the shore. So the old woman had held him captive with her garrulousness, she thought irritably. Oh why, why she asked herself, when Neil was so taciturn should his mother be such a blather?

The smell of cooking fish was wafting appetizingly through the open door and when Catriona entered she found the young man seated at the table enjoying a plate of fish and hot buttered scones. She bit her lip. In no way did she begrudge her mother-in-law's hospitality but she was vexed that the young man was still around and, from the look of the situation, seemed likely to be around for a while longer.

The old woman shot her a defiant glance. 'The young Englishman is hungry,' she explained, 'and he did not know how to cook the fish you gave him.'

'The sea makes one hungry,' Catriona conceded. She felt awkward in the young man's presence and since she hated eating in front of strangers she was disconcerted when her mother-in-law put a plate of fish on the table and pushed it towards her. Reluctantly she sat down.

'I can honestly say I've never enjoyed fish so much in my life,' the young man enthused. 'You don't know how lucky you are to be able to just go out and catch a fish or two for your meal whenever you feel like it.'

'It's not always so easy,' Catriona pointed out. 'It depends on the weather.' Her resentment towards him began to lessen a little. 'And it depends on the fish,' she added with a faint smile.

'Naturally,' he agreed, returning her smile. 'What do you call these fish, by the way?'

'Sooyan, is what we call them but I can't give you the English for them,' she replied. 'You are English?'

'That's right. Yorkshire English. Sorry, I should have introduced myself before. My name's Jones.'

'Chones,' repeated the old woman. 'And you will be a doctor?' she surmised. She always flattered strangers by implying they were grand enough to be members of one of the professions.

'Good gracious, no! I'm a car salesman normally but when I'm on holiday I join up with a friend of mine who, like me, likes to go birdwatching. He's the owner of the boat out there but he had an urgent call to go back to his job for a few days to do a bit of sorting out. I'm picking him up again at Oban.'

'You go birdwatching?' The old woman was suddenly full of interest. 'Aye well, it's many a bird you'll see on this island that you might not see in England no matter how hard you look.'

'No great northern divers?' he inquired hopefully, and when both Catriona and the old woman shook their heads he went on, 'Now that's a bird I'd really like to see. I've not been lucky enough yet, though. It's said to nest up here but my friend and I haven't found one so far.'

'No, indeed,' the old woman consoled him. 'I've never heard tell of a great northern diver nesting on this island. But we have storm petrels that nest here. My own son knows all there is to know about the island and he found a petrel colony over by the Bheinn Mhor,' she declared.

Catriona was aghast. Neil had found the rare petrel colony and had taken her and the cailleach there to see and hear the petrels for themselves, but wishing to protect the colony from intruders he had sworn both her and his mother to secrecy about his discovery. What had come over the old woman that she was now babbling out the cherished secret to a total stranger? Why, for all she knew he might be an egg collector! She tried to glower her mother-in-law into silence.

'A petrel colony? Here on the island?' The young man looked excitedly at Catriona. She avoided his eyes. 'Do you know where it is? Can you take me there?'

'Why, surely Catriona knows where it is,' the old woman assured him, and ignoring Catriona's stricken expression she went on, 'If only my son was here he would be pleased to take you to see the place. But Catriona will take you, will you not, Catriona? Seeing Mister Chones must be away in his boat tomorrow it would be a shame for him not to be able to see the petrels.'

Anger flashed through Catriona. Neil would have some very strong words to say to his mother when he returned. She looked down at her plate.

'I'd be most grateful if you'd show me the colony.' His voice was pleading. 'It really would be the highlight of my holiday. According to my records there's no mention of a petrel colony on this island.'

'It has been a secret for a long time,' Catriona rebuffed him.

'It will still be a secret, I promise you. You have my word of honour that I won't speak of it to a soul,' he said earnestly.

His word of honour, Catriona thought cynically. What respect would a 'here today and gone tomorrow' Englishman have for a word of honour?

'Tonight will be a good night for the petrels,' the old woman insisted. 'No moon and plenty of dim but no darkness and the wind still as a bog. Surely it would be a great shame for Mister Chones to miss such a sight.' She looked compellingly at Catriona. 'Surely you will do that for him,' she said confidently.

'You're not an egg collector?' Catriona challenged him.

'Certainly not!' he replied indignantly.

She felt she could no longer demur. She had no wish to take the young man to the petrel colony; no wish for his company; least of all no wish to betray Neil's discovery. But the old woman was so pressing she had no doubt Neil would understand that under the circumstances courtesy had required her to defer to his mother's insistence. 'Very well, I will take you,' she said. 'Just as soon as you're ready.'

The night was mild and moonless. The purple sea was still patched with the afterglow of sunset. The outer islands were fuzzy dark shapes on the horizon. Catriona set a pace brisk enough to discourage conversation until, nearing the site of the colony, she slowed.

The young man paused and laid an arresting hand on her arm. 'Are we near them?' he whispered. 'I thought for a moment I was hearing something.'

'I am smelling them,' she retorted nimbly. He pressed her arm companionably. As they proceeded slowly his hand slid down to hers, wanting her to share his excitement. She did not try to draw her hand away.

Catriona's alert ears detected a faint churring. 'Listen!' she murmured commandingly.

The faint churring grew louder and louder and then as they breasted a low hillock the air was suddenly filled with the seemingly weightless shapes of the petrels flying with swift batlike aimlessness and patterning the starless sky like wind-whipped leaves.

The young man squeezed her hand. 'God! But this is stupendous!' he exclaimed, his tone reflecting his awe.

He was standing perfectly still as if transfixed by the sight, and Catriona, touched by his obvious enthusiasm, let herself be caught up in the excitement. Urging him towards a cluster of raised hummocks she knelt and put her ear to the ground, beckoning him to do likewise, and when she saw the mounting rapturousness of his expression as he listened to the squeaks and scrabblings of the nestlings in their underground nursery her sense of guilt at betraying Neil's secret retreated temporarily .

She waited patiently until he rose. 'Now that you have not only seen them but heard them and smelled them it is time we went back,' she said, and turned to lead the way. But the young man did not move.

'Catriona, let's stay here until the birds go back to sea,' he begged eagerly. 'Please. It's doubtful if I'll ever get the chance to witness something like this again so I'd like to see it through to the end.'

She shrugged acceptance. It would be little more than an hour before the petrels would be departing to spend the daylight hours at sea, and since she was not tired she had no wish to curtail his pleasure by insisting on an immediate return. They settled themselves on a mossy incline, their backs against a smooth granite boulder.

'This,' proclaimed the young man, 'will undoubtedly rank as the most memorable experience of my birdwatching life. And it's all thanks to you, Catriona.' He reached for her hand and pressed it to his lips.

The gesture startled her and she had to stifle a giggle as she quickly pulled her hand away. It was a totally new experience for her to have her hand kissed and the absurdity of his action lit such a spark of merriment in her eyes that she had to stare steadily at the sea to give time for the amusement to fade from her expression. What fools these English men were, she told herself. 'You should be thanking the cailleach,' she disputed. 'I would never have told you of the place, let alone brought you here.'

'I could see that well enough,' he acknowledged. 'Tell me, what is this word "cailleach" you use? Is it the Gaelic for grandmother?'

'For grandmother, mother, old woman or indeed any woman with age on her. It can be a term of endearment just as easily as it can be a term of scorn. It is difficult to explain,' she told him.

He lay back and drew up his knees. 'I certainly count myself a lucky man tonight,' he said.

'Indeed,' she agreed. 'The petrels don't come in such numbers every night.'

'I don't mean just seeing the petrel colony but seeing them in the company of a girl as fresh and beautiful as yourself, Catriona.' He rolled on his side the better to study her.

A tremor of apprehension ran through her and yet she knew she need not be afraid of him. 'Now you are talking foolish nonsense,' she rebuked him.

'I am not,' he contradicted. 'You have a splendidly wild beauty, Catriona. Mesmerizing, I should say. Has no one ever told you so?' A kind of fervour crept into his voice.

The embarrassment she had felt on first seeing him returned. She steadied her voice. 'You must stop talking such nonsense or you will be making me think you are drunk or have gone off your head so it is not safe for me to be with you. I have a good mind to leave you here to find your own way back,' she threatened, pursing her lips so they could not soften into a smile. He was indeed foolish, she thought, but all the same it was pleasant to hear such things.

With a pretended groan he lay back and turned away from her. 'I feel I'm drunk,' he admitted. 'Drunk with excitement.' For some time there was a silence between them and then he said, 'I say, Catriona, I've got a terrible thirst on me. Is there a stream or a pool nearby where I can get a drink?'

She was about to reply that there was a stream some distance away but she stopped herself. A small imp of recklessness lurking at the back of her mind told her she now had an opportunity to revenge herself for the embarrassment he had caused her, first with his nakedness and then for having manoeuvred her into bringing him here and disturbing her with his foolish talk. 'Over this way,' she said, guiding him towards a small spring that cascaded over moss-covered rocks.

Eagerly the young man lay down and let the flow pour into his mouth and over his face. The next moment he sprang to his feet, coughing and spitting. Catriona moved a few steps away, unable to control her laughter. He lurched towards her.

'God! Are you trying to poison me?' he demanded.

'It's perfectly good water,' she told him, stepping adroitly out of his reach. 'And it is very good for the stomach. It is to this spring we come when we need medicine.'

'You minx!' he upbraided her. 'I've a jolly good mind to force a dose of it down your own throat this very minute.' Before she could evade him he had rushed forward, and grabbing her arms, had begun pulling her towards the spring. As she twisted and fought against his grip she stumbled and fell. The next moment they were together on the ground, gasping and laughing as they struggled with each other. 'My, but you're strong as well as beautiful,' he complimented her breathlessly.

'You're not so weak yourself,' she told him. 'You can let me go now.' But instead of relaxing his hold his hands pinioned her shoulders. He bent over her.

'I would like very much to kiss you, Catriona,' he said.

'There has already been too much foolishness between us,' she told him severely, wriggling her shoulders against his grip. He made no move to release her and as her own hands pushed him away she could feel his flesh beneath the thin shirt; not sweaty flesh such as Neil's would have been but having a vibrant warmth that made her own fingers tingle in response. She knew at that moment what was likely to happen. She also knew that had she exerted her full strength against him she could almost certainly have freed herself, but he was young and he was foolish and she had no wish to hurt him.

He held her face, forcing her to look up at him, and she tried to feign an angry expression, but they looked too long into each other's eyes. His mouth fastened on her lips and then moved gently over her face and closed her eyelids and as he lifted his body to cover hers she knew she wanted to yield to what, to her, was an entirely new and exciting kind of 'cuddling', which was her term for lovemaking. When he began pulling urgently at her clothes and she felt the coolness of the moss under her bare buttocks her body was already quivering with acquiescence.

23

* * *

An hour later they were watching the petrels flighting back to sea.

'A night of total enchantment,' the young man commented feelingly and seemed inclined to linger, but Catriona was impatient to start for home. He tried to take her arm but now she drew away from him and if she saw his rueful glance she ignored it.

'Ready?' she said curtly, and again walking ahead of him she strode briskly homewards. As they were nearing the gate to the croft she paused and, turning to him, said, 'I wish you to swear once more to me that you will never, ever tell any living soul of the petrel colony you have seen here.'

For a moment he looked dumbfounded. 'The petrel colony?' he repeated, as if he had been expecting her to make an entirely different request. 'I promised you, didn't I? And I reckon I keep my word. All the same it's a pity you want to keep it to yourselves. I'm certain it would be of tremendous interest to ornithologists to know there is a colony here. Why do you not want anyone to know?'

'Because the cailleach did wrong to mention it to you. It is not her secret but her son's. When he discovered it he told her and swore her to secrecy. Even I was not aware of it until after I was married. It is my husband's secret and should remain so till he chooses to tell of it.'

'Your husband? Did I hear you say your husband?' He was gaping at her in consternation. Catriona stared at him unblinkingly. 'You're married?' He was almost stammering with incredulity. When she nodded affirmation his manner changed hastily. 'Where is your husband?'

'Did you not hear my mother-in-law tell you that her son was away from home until next week?'

He looked stunned. 'That old woman you call the cailleach is your mother-in-law? Dear God! I took her to be your grandmother at least!' He glanced down at her hands. 'You don't wear a wedding ring,' he accused.

'On the Sabbath only,' she told him. 'It is the custom.'

'That's that then,' he said. 'I'm clearing out as fast as I can, so I don't suppose I shall see you again.'

24

'It is unlikely.' Her tone was coolly dismissive.

'Well, all that's left for me to say is thank you for an unusual and interesting evening's entertainment,' he said caustically. He started to move away and then paused. 'Why couldn't you have told me you were married?' he demanded plaintively. For answer she looked at him with puzzled inquiry. With a muffled comment he turned and went striding down to the shore and, she assumed, out of her life.

It was too early to start the morning's work so Catriona went to bed and slept until wakened by the calves bawling to be fed. When she rose the yacht had gone from the bay.

It was best so, she told herself dispassionately. She felt no guilt after her indiscretion of the previous evening. It had been a natural thing to happen to a man and a woman alone in the semi-darkness and silence of the moors. She had not planned it to happen. Had not expected it to happen, since she had started off by disliking the young man. It was the cailleach who had been responsible by insisting that the young man should see the petrels. It was finished now and she felt no regret that the young man had gone; no lingering attraction, in fact no emotion whatsoever save when in the ensuing months she occasionally recalled her experience with a kind of saucy satisfaction.

She was eating her porridge when the cailleach appeared. The old woman filled a bowl and sat down at the table but she had taken only a couple of spoonfuls before she put her spoon down and looked anxiously at her daughter-in-law. 'You will not say to Neil that I forgot my promise to him and told the young man about the petrels?' she pleaded. 'He will say I am a stupid old woman and no longer to be trusted.'

'You were indeed a stupid old woman, cailleach!' Catriona scolded her. The cailleach looked abject. 'Very well, I will not speak to him of it,' Catriona relented. 'We will not speak of the young man's visit at all. But you must be sure and never tell anyone else,' she insisted. 'You shamed me into taking the young man there since I could not refuse without being rude. And would you or Neil or indeed my own mother wish me to show anything but kindness to a stranger? Isn't that the way it has always been on this island?' she finished indignantly. The old woman flicked her a look of gratitude as she murmured vague agreement.

The following evening when Catriona came back to the cottage after finishing her chores she noticed a trace of excitement in the old woman's manner. As soon as Catriona sat down the old woman, thrusting her hand into the pocket of her apron, produced a bottle of gingery-coloured liquid.

'I was after visiting old Flora McNamus yesterday and I got this dose from her. She said I was to give it to you and it would help you to have a bairn.' The old woman's hand shook a little as she held out the bottle. 'Will you not try it?' she begged when Catriona seemed heedless of her suggestion.

Old Flora McNamus was supposed to possess all kinds of magical powers and at one time, before doctors and nurses had become easier to contact, she had been called upon to concoct all kinds of potions and medicines for both people and animals. Her cures were still reputed by many to outmatch modern medicines and there had been times during the past year when Catriona herself had felt desperate enough to think of paying old Flora a secret visit. She took the bottle and after shaking it held it up to the light. 'A dose night and morning,' the old woman said.

Catriona grimaced sceptically. 'I will try it,' she said, her lukewarm tone disguising her eagerness. She took her first dose that night.

She was glad when Neil returned the following week. She had missed him in every way. Without his burly frame the cottage had seemed empty. Without his strong firm body beside her in the bed she had felt isolated. Her eyes glowed as she waited for him to come up from the shore. She loved her husband. He and he only was her man; her satisfying true lover who cuddled her stolidly in the way she had grown used to being cuddled.

As she snuggled up to him on the night of his return she wondered mischievously what his reaction might be were she one day to summon up enough courage to suggest to him that he should stand before her naked; or ask him why they should not cuddle on a summer evening in some solitary place on the moors rather than in the secrecy of their bed? In the safety of the darkness she let an impish smile play around her mouth.

Three months after Neil's return from Glasgow Catriona knew beyond doubt that she was pregnant. She was ecstatic. Her mind was brimful of anticipation; her hands busy with preparations. Neil's normally impassive expression softened to one of serenity. His old mother seemed to find that the prospect of a grandchild gave her renewed strength.

When the baby, a lusty boy, arrived Catriona showed him proudly to her husband. 'He's certainly been worth waiting for,' he commented.

The old woman was quick to appoint herself nurse and was content to sit for most of the day in her chair, crooning and clucking to the gurgling baby in her lap. Catriona, busy enough with the spring work of the croft, was glad to have it so for it was becoming plain to both her and Neil that his mother was becoming more frail. The surge of energy which had manifested itself when Catriona had announced that she was pregnant seemed gradually to have dissipated and by the time the spring work had come to an end she had become so vague and forgetful that Catriona, worrying about her ability to cope with the child, found herself having to spend much more time around the house.

She was at home one day engaged in the daily nappy washing when her mother-in-law gave a slight moan and leaned forward in her chair. Catriona went quickly to her side. The old woman was breathing quickly and Catriona wondered if she should run and get someone to go for the nurse, but instead she held a glass of whisky to her lips and within half an hour her mother-in-law had recovered sufficiently to be able to assure her that there was nothing wrong with her save a bout of indigestion. She asked for the child to be put in her lap.

Catriona, watchfully complying, said indulgently, 'It is spoiling the bairn you are with all your petting, cailleach.'

'I could not be petting and loving him more were he my own son's bairn,' her mother-in-law said.

Catriona, assuming the old woman's mind was wandering, said, 'Surely he is your own son's bairn, cailleach.' The old woman shook her head. 'Then are ye thinking the fairies have visited us and substituted some changeling for our own child?' Catriona teased, and thought how amused Neil would be when she told him of his mother's strange talk. 'Why are you nursing him so lovingly if he is not truly your own grandchild? My child and Neil's?' she pursued, her voice edged with scorn.

'Indeed he is truly your child,' the old woman replied. 'But I am telling you he is not the child of my son's loins.' Catriona stared at her, certain that her mother-in-law had taken leave of her senses. She was about to utter a sharp rebuke when the old woman went on. 'My son can never father a child though he does not and must never know it,' she asserted. 'It is a sad thing but it is something that comes through my family – through my mother and my grandmother and her mother and grandmothers before her as far back as anyone can remember. It is a curse some say was laid upon us by a witch long ago. We women can have children but no son of ours can father children.'

'That's nonsense!' Catriona snapped, her tolerance gone.

'It is not nonsense. It is true, right enough. My other son, Neil's brother who was killed in the war, was married eight years before he died but there was no bairn. My own mother's sister's son has been married these thirty years but he has no family, though he and his wife longed for a bairn. There is no doubting the curse is still on us.'

'But don't you remember, cailleach,' Catriona reminded her. 'It was Flora McNamus's dose that helped give me the child. Surely you cannot have forgotten getting the dose for me? Ach!' she added derisively, 'It is mad you are.' She made to go out into the larder.

Again the old woman shook her head and, reaching out, detained Catriona by laying a hand on her arm. 'It was not the dose that helped you to have the bairn. I wanted you to believe that at the time but indeed it could not have been so.

I must tell you now because I am old and must soon pass on. The father of your bairn is surely the young man you took to see the petrels. Mister Chones. That could be so, could it not?'

Catriona's stupefied gaze stayed riveted on her mother-in-law. Again she protested, 'That is nonsense. The bairn is the image of Neil, everyone can see the likeness. I cannot believe that Neil is not his father.'

'Your son is fair like Neil, but tell me, wasn't the young man you took to see the petrels also fair?'

Catriona covered her burning face with her hands. 'But if what you are saying is true then I am wicked. Truly wicked!' she sobbed.

The shrewd old eyes were on her. 'Is it so wicked for a woman to give her man the bairn he is wanting?'

'But you say Neil is not the father . . .' Catriona's voice trailed into disbelief once more.

'That he must never know.' The old woman was as emphatic as her frail body would allow. 'Neil is a proud man and the shame of knowing that he could not father bairns would destroy him.' She shook her daughter-in-law's arm, stressing the importance of what she was saying. 'It is the woman always who must be blamed for childlessness.'

Catriona shook her head bemusedly. 'It cannot be true. It cannot,' she insisted, though with lessening conviction.

'It is true,' the old woman reiterated. 'What mother would be cruel enough to say such a thing if it was not so?'

'Dear God!' Catriona whispered. 'I hardly remember him.' She had indeed banished the young man easily enough from her memory but now his presence was there asserting itself as if he were in the room. She sagged to her knees beside the old woman's chair, her face hidden in her clasped hands. 'What have I done?' she wailed. A moment later she looked up at the old woman accusingly. 'Was it your doing, cailleach? Was it your design to shame me into taking the young man to see the petrels?'

'It was best so,' comforted the old woman. 'The outcome is a happy one, is it not?' She studied Catriona's face. 'Together now we must keep this secret between us. I swear to you there is no happier way.' She gripped Catriona's wrist with all the strength she could muster.

'But if what you are saying is true there can be no more bairns,' Catriona whimpered tragically.

The old woman stroked her daughter-in-law's bent head. 'One bairn has given my son great happiness,' she reasoned. 'It is for you and you only to decide whether more bairns would increase his happiness.'

'But how can I?' Catriona exclaimed miserably. 'It's impossible.'

'You love Neil?'

Catriona was unsure whether it was a question or a statement. 'Of course I do,' she was quick to affirm. 'I would do anything to make Neil happy.'

'That is what I hoped you would say,' her mother-in-law said complacently. She looked fondly at the child and then slid her work-roughened fingers under Catriona's chin, turning her face so they were forced to look into each other's eyes. 'You are a bonny lass and will be so for many years to come,' she told her. 'And the petrels are known to be faithful to their nesting places.' Her voice sank confidingly. 'And is this place not truly called the Bay of Strangers,' she whispered, 'and do we not say here that the truth belongs only to God?'

2

The Banjimolly

I had been driving for more than two hours, hunched over
the steering wheel, peering through the constantly fogging
windscreen while the wipers strove to contend with the
sluicing Highland rain which had already turned every rut
of the twisting, sharp-flinted road into a runnel, every
pothole into a puddle. Changing down to negotiate an
intimidatingly wide puddle beyond which the road began to
rear steeply, I was dismayed to hear the engine race, lose
power and then, after one or two faintly promising surges,
die completely.

Muttering epithets and entreaties I tried several times to
re-start it, but fearing the battery would become exhausted
I gave up and putting the car into neutral, let her run back a
few yards to where a slightly wider curve in the road would,
I hoped, prevent her from being a hazard to any other traffic
there might be. Unwilling to risk opening the bonnet in
such a downpour – unwilling even to open the door of the
car – I sat and watched the rolling screen of rain fill the
landscape while I kept my ears alert so as to detect the first
sound of an approaching engine above the noise of the rain
hammering relentlessly on the roof.

It was a long and worrying twenty minutes before the
welcome sound came, and getting out of the car I signalled
pleadingly as a small van emerged from the mist and gloom.
With creakings and grindings it pulled up beside me.

'Gone bad on you, has she?' The driver's face puckered
against the rain as he leaned out to call to me.

He came over and I moved into the passenger seat while he
fiddled with the switches and tried unsuccessfully to
persuade the engine into life. 'I'll have to get out and look at
her,' he said, and borrowing the travelling rug from the

back of the car to protect both himself and the engine, he opened the bonnet.

Reluctantly I too got out of the car and stood beside him, getting wetter and wetter as I watched him probe and prod, not very reassuringly I thought, at various parts of the engine. Finally, after again trying the ignition, he shook his head. Closing the bonnet, he stood for a moment surveying the car perplexedly.

'Will you give me a lift to the nearest garage or telephone?' I asked as he handed me back the now sodden travelling rug.

He looked a little nonplussed. 'The trouble is I have a patient in the back of the van that I'm taking home from the hospital. I'd best do that first but her place is only a couple of miles further on, so if you like I'll drop her off first and then on my way back I'll pick you up and take you to my cousin's garage.' He nodded in the direction from which he had come. 'It's no more than four miles back and he'll surely be able to fix your car for you in no time at all.'

I had lived too long in the Highlands to be more than momentarily shocked by the disclosure that a newly discharged hospital patient was being taken home in the back of an almost clapped-out van rather than in an ambulance. Some good reason for it would undoubtedly emerge, I told myself, and was getting back into my car when the driver called again.

'You could always come along with me,' he invited. 'Likely it will be warmer for you here in the van than sitting waiting in your car.'

It sounded a good idea, so collecting my handbag and the ignition key I left the car and got into the van beside the driver.

'Thank goodness you came along,' I remarked as I settled into the seat.

'Aye, you could have been there all night,' he agreed with instant sympathy.

'And I'm glad you offered to take me along with you,' I added. 'It would have been a cold and dreary wait.'

'To tell the truth I might be glad of your company,' he

replied with a wry smile. Gesturing with his thumb over his shoulder, he went on, 'Seeing the old woman I have in the back is supposed to be a witch.'

'A witch?' I returned his smile.

'Aye. The Banjimolly they call her hereabouts. I don't believe in such things myself,' he repudiated, 'but there's plenty of the old folks reckoned her grandmother and her mother before her were witches, so she'll likely have the power still.'

'Banjimolly,' I murmured reflectively. 'Is it a Gaelic word?'

'Aye, I believe it could be, though I haven't a word of the language myself.'

'Is Banjimolly the patient you spoke of?' I asked.

'Aye. You see, what happened was, the hospital hadn't a spare ambulance to come out all this way so they hired a car to take her back to her home,' he explained. 'Then didn't the car break down just the other side of my cousin's garage and when my cousin had looked over it he said it would take a while before he could get it going again. The driver was in a terrible rush to get back and Banjimolly was there cursing and swearing at having to wait. In the end my cousin couldn't stand it so he sent a message to me asking would I take the old woman home in my van while he took the driver back in the car he uses as a taxi.' As if suspecting I was on the point of questioning this seemingly callous arrangement, he resumed, 'See, my cousin's wife is terrible superstitious and she swore she'd never set foot in any car after Banjimolly had been near it. She reckoned she'd put a spell on it or something. So there was nothing for it but to put the old woman in the van.' There was the merest trace of penitence in his tone. 'It's maybe not so comfortable for her as the car would have been, but knowing the place she lives in I don't reckon she'll notice.'

We drove on for a few minutes before I asked, 'You're not superstitious yourself then?'

'Ach, Banjimolly's no witch,' he responded contemptuously. 'She's nothing but a crazy old woman.'

Hardly had he finished speaking when the van hit a

flooded pothole, jolting me so that my head came in ungentle contact with the roof. At the same time from behind the partition came a loud and persistent wailing. The driver and I exchanged glances.

'Oh God!' he exclaimed. 'I suppose I'll have to go and see what's gone with her now.'

He got out and went to investigate and as the rear doors opened I could hear his voice, questioning and chiding, interspersed by another voice shrilling with what sounded like accusation and complaint. I went to see if I could be of any help.

Banjimolly, both of her legs encased in mummy-like bandages, lay half crouched on the floor of the van, obviously having been dislodged from the makeshift mattress on which she was supposed to be lying. Her appearance surprised me. Undoubtedly she was old but in no way did she resemble my idea of a witch. She wasn't even a withered old crone, as I would have expected, but was rather plump and smooth-skinned. There was nothing alarming about her save that her brown eyes were bright with hostility as she glared at the driver, denouncing him with ear-stinging vituperation while she struggled to regain her position on the mattress. While her back was towards us she failed to notice the driver wink at me and reach forward to pick up a half bottle of whisky, empty but for a few dregs.

'D'you think she's hurt?' I whispered.

'Not her,' he muttered. 'She's shouting because she dropped her whisky when we hit that pothole and she's spilled the lot, so she says. More likely she's drunk the most of it first.'

Catching sight of me, the old woman ceased her gabblings and began to moan. She pressed a hand to her heart and her eyes closed as her head drooped forward.

'Oh, I'm sure she must be hurt,' I told the driver and, panic-stricken, ran to get the as yet unopened half bottle of whisky which I had providently slipped into my handbag at the commencement of my journey. After taking off the cap I held out the bottle towards her. Instantly, despite apparently closed eyes, the old woman saw it.

Her lids flicked wide, and darting me a quick glance from under scowling brows, she stretched out a twitching, covetous hand to grasp it.

There was a suppressed exclamation from the driver as he watched her swallow several mouthfuls. I sensed rather than heard his agonized protest when I told her to keep the remainder of the bottle.

'Oh, but surely that's too good of you, my dear. Too good indeed. It's so awful kind of you I couldn't be taking it from you,' the old woman demurred though she still clutched the bottle possessively. 'Such a good, kind lady,' she repeated when I insisted.

'Are you all right now?' the driver demanded testily, and hardly waiting for her grunted reply he slammed and fastened the doors.

'Bloody waste of good whisky on a mad old woman like that,' he rebuked me when we were back in our seats. 'That's the best brand of whisky a man can buy. It would frighten you to know the cost of even a half bottle of that stuff.' He caught my glance. 'You didn't buy it yourself, surely?' His tone implied that he thought me incapable of such discriminating taste.

I confessed I had bought it; that indeed the price had frightened me but that I had been persuaded to buy it by a friend, a connoisseur, who, on hearing that I regarded whisky as a medicine – effective though unpleasant – had recommended I should try this particular brand, assuring me that it was like drinking velvet steeped in liquid sunshine.

'That's true, right enough,' concurred the driver reverently.

I wondered what he would say if he knew I had bought not one but two half bottles. The second one was still in the suitcase in my car.

When we reached her cottage the driver and I helped Banjimolly out of the van, whereupon the driver – with the rather flimsy excuse that the road was too narrow just there to turn the van so he would have to drive on a little way and find a better turning place – left me to cope with the old woman on my own.

She spurned my proffered arm and used her stick to aid her along the muddy path.

'Thank goodness the rain has eased off at last,' I said as I walked beside her.

At the door of her dreary-looking cottage she turned and, grasping my hand, she shook it repeatedly, emphasizing yet again that she would never forget my kindness. 'Tell me,' she wanted to know, 'how much further will the driver be taking you before you reach the place you are wanting to go?'

Realizing that the van had only a roof-light in the back and therefore she would not have seen my broken-down car, I explained my plight telling her that the driver was now going to take me back to his cousin's garage where I could expect to get help of one sort or another.

'Aye and the rascal will charge you for it,' she warned. I shrugged acceptance. She looked hard at me, her eyes narrowing. 'I'll cure your car for you,' she said, startlingly.

'I think . . .' I began but she cut me short.

'You have with you the key it takes to start her?' I nodded. 'Let me take a look at it,' she demanded. When I hesitated her voice took on a note of whining reproval. 'Will you no be letting Banjimolly take a wee look at your key? Surely an old woman can do it no harm and sometimes Banjimolly can cure when others cannot,' she added with a curiously sly look.

Deciding to humour her, I displayed the ignition key on the palm of my hand, watching her closely as she took it between her thumb and forefinger. Her fingers closed over it and her clenched hand began to circle the air, slowly at first then more rapidly. At the same time she blew out her lips, making a burring sound such as a small boy would make trying to imitate the noise of an engine. After several moments of disquiet when I feared she might be going to hurl my key away, making me hunt for it on the rushy ground, I could feel only embarrassment at the absurdity of her performance. The driver was all too right about Banjimolly being crazy, I thought.

She straightened and her eyes looked calmly into the

distance about six inches above my head for a few moments. She handed me back my key. 'I have cured your car,' she said dismissively. 'You will have no need to get help to make it go.'

'Thank you very much,' I managed to say. Before going indoors she paused to ask my name. I told her and started to hurry back to the van.

'Banjimolly will always remember you!' she called after me. 'Banjimolly never forgets a kindness.'

'My, but you were a whiley with the old woman,' the driver commented. 'What was she saying to you?'

'She told me she'd cured my car,' I said, my voice breaking into a chuckle. 'She says I won't need help to get it going.'

'Ach!' His tone was eloquent. All the same when we came in sight of my car he slowed the van. 'Do you want to stop and try her, then?' he asked in a combative way.

'Why not?' I responded.

'Ach, I doubt it's no use,' he said but as soon as I turned the key in the ignition the engine reacted.

'Well, I'm damned!' said the driver as he leaned on the window. 'What did you do to her?'

'I simply switched her on,' I said. We looked at each other in astonishment and delight.

'That's a mystery right enough,' he admitted, his brow creased with doubt.

'Maybe Banjimolly is really a witch and she did put a spell on it,' I suggested flippantly.

'Damty sure there's no witch had a hand in it,' he asserted. I laughed and revved the engine into exultant life. 'Are you going to trust to luck that she'll keep going?' he inquired.

I felt reckless. 'Yes,' I replied. 'She sounds healthy enough, doesn't she?' His nod was one of puzzled affirmation. I steered the car back on to the road. 'If I can get as far as the next village I shall be all right,' I told him. 'I have friends there.'

'I'd best follow you for a whiley just to make sure she keeps going,' the driver volunteered.

'I'd be very grateful if you'd do that,' I rejoined. With a twinge of regret I reached into the back of the car and extracted the second half bottle of whisky from my suitcase. 'Do have this.' I handed it to him. 'I don't suppose I should ever have got around to drinking it.'

He gaped and then smiled with pleasure. 'Are you sure? Honestly?' he exclaimed, though his fingers were already intent on opening it. 'Are you sure you won't take a wee dram yourself first?' His tone was dissuasive and he was obviously delighted by my refusal.

My car purred along unfalteringly, but true to his word the driver continued to follow me for some miles before I heard a farewell blast on his horn and saw in my driving mirror that he was turning for home. Confidently I carried on. The rain had ceased altogether now and the evening sky was showing faint traces of pink.

When without further shilly-shallyings I arrived at my own cottage my neighbour, ever curious about my comings and goings, came hurrying over.

'You're late!' she greeted me. 'I was after being feared you'd broken down some place.'

'I did break down for a while,' I admitted.

'Oh, my! And in such weather as there's been,' she commiserated. And then after a pause she asked, 'Would it be a bit of the engine that went wrong then?'

Since my neighbour's knowledge of engines was limited to their being composed entirely of 'bits' – and since, being in her eighties, she was unlikely ever to pursue a more intimate acquaintance with them – I felt no compunction when I told her, 'No. All it needed was a little Banjimolly treatment.'

Though a Gaelic speaker she evidently did not connect my pronunciation of 'Banjimolly' with any word in that language. 'Oh, indeed,' she said vaguely. 'That would have been a costly thing to have done, I reckon?'

'Oh no,' I began but then I stopped, remembering those two half bottles of 'velvet steeped in liquid sunshine'. I smiled a small, secret smile. 'Well it wasn't cheap,' I allowed, 'but I think it was worth it. In a way I'm inclined to regard it as being a kind of insurance.'

3

Island Encounter

Ducking her head to avoid the low stone lintel, Katy emerged from the gloom of the byre and, putting down the empty feeding pails, shut the door on the disgruntled calves and their greedy protestations that they were still hungry. She threaded the makeshift rope handle through the hole in the door and knotted it tightly before turning to scan the broad apron of the bay, where the calm waters were still touched with the gold of the tarrying evening sunlight. Evidently reassured by what she saw she picked up the pails and sped lightly back to the cottage. Keeping the bay under observation while she scoured the pails and sluiced the waste water on to the cobbled path, she noted the first cat's-paws of breeze which were beginning to stroke the water into its predictable evening restlessness. Something caught her eye, and deserting her task temporarily she ran towards a crag of rock on which she climbed so as to get a better view of the shore. Her clear grey eyes narrowed as she discerned a figure labouring to shift the storm-tumbled boulders so as to make a clearway down to the water wide enough for the passage of a small dinghy which, though she could not see it, she knew lay high above the tide line of wrack. Hastily Katy finished the scouring and went into the cottage.

'Sandy passed by a wee whiley since and left word for you that he's going fishing,' her mother greeted her.

'I was thinking he would do that,' Katy replied. 'I'll need to make haste and take my tea,' she added.

'Ach, time enough,' her mother said. 'I see no sign of a change in the weather.'

Though the sun had now disappeared behind the distant hill peaks it was the time of the year when, unless masked by rain clouds, daylight spun itself out to last almost the whole of the twenty-four hours. There would be light enough to fish all night if they felt so inclined, Katy concluded.

'Sandy's already away down to the shore,' she told her mother. 'He'll not be so pleased if I keep him waiting.'

Lifting the girdle from the fire, her mother slid fresh-baked scones on to the clean towel which lay in readiness to receive them. Katy meanwhile filled a cup from the teapot on the hob and, sitting down, sipped cautiously at the hot tea and watched absently while her mother sliced a wedge of home-made butter and laid it in the centre of a scone before topping it with a spoonful of crowdie. Reaching out, Katy took it from her and, skilfully tilting it in her fingers, coaxed the melting butter to circle the crowdie before it spread over the whole scone. She bit into it hungrily. 'Where's Cassy?' she asked.

Her mother looked up from her baking. 'Why now, but where would you expect her to be at this hour?' she retorted. 'Isn't she in the room there getting herself changed as she always does for the evening?' She nodded meaningly towards the door between the kitchen and the bedroom.

Katy smiled but made no comment.

Cassy, her cousin from Glasgow, was paying her first visit to the island – a visit insisted upon by her father who, though he had been born on the island, had left it to make a career in the city. He was now a successful businessman and a few weeks previously he had written expressing a wish that his only child, Cassy, should come and see for herself his humble birthplace.

From the moment her mother had first mentioned the proposed visit Katy had found herself looking forward with a mixture of excitement and disquiet to meeting her Glasgow cousin. It would undoubtedly be strange at first since not only had they never met but they had not even corresponded. She had mentioned her moments of disquiet to her mother.

'Ach, but you're kinsmen and you're both of an age,

lassie. I doubt you're bound to have plenty in common, different though you may be at first,' her mother had assured her.

And so it had proved to be, though Katy's first glimpse of the slender, colourfully attired figure who had coquettishly demanded the support of the ferryman's strong arms before she would step ashore, had filled her with awe. Her first thought was that her cousin could easily have modelled for one of the elegant figures depicted in their mail-order catalogue from which they rarely purchased but over which they frequently pored, or even for one of the heroines portrayed in the much-thumbed romantic story magazines which came into the house from time to time. Katy had been prepared for meeting someone much different from herself; she had not been prepared for meeting someone who struck her as being quite so beautiful and so elegant. Beside her cousin, Katy had been instantly aware of her own dowdiness, while in the presence of Cassy's easy manners and insouciant laughter she had felt gauche and tongue-tied.

Later in the bedroom they were to share, she had watched bemusedly as her cousin had unpacked one glamorous but totally unsuitable garment after another. Too shy to comment, she had confined herself to smiling admiringly though her mind was questioning when on earth Cassy expected to wear such clothes. She was soon to find out.

In the earlier part of the day Cassy had appeared in the customary tourist attire of tweeds and brogues or, on a rare day of warmth, in dresses and sandals, but as evening approached – a time she judged not by the light but by the time the scholars were released from school, she would change into what she referred to as 'afternoon clothes', which, since they were usually too flimsy to give her protection from the sea-chilled evenings, compelled her to sit close to the fire until she was ready to go to bed. Even after she had come to accept that there was simply nowhere to go on the island save the homes of neighbours where the end of the day's chores was acknowledged, if at all, only by the women putting on clean aprons, Cassy had not been deterred from the ritual of changing.

'Surely she's kind of late dressing herself this evening, is she not?' Katy observed to her mother with amused interest. 'Is she thinking she's going somewhere special?'

'Indeed, is she not coming fishing with yourself and Sandy,' her mother responded with surprise.

Katy looked up, startled for a moment until she decided her mother was teasing her. 'I'm sure Cassy would not be wanting to come fishing with us,' she repudiated with a chuckle.

'I'm thinking she's set on it,' insisted her mother.

'But who on earth would put that idea into her head? Surely Sandy didn't ask her?'

'Sandy didn't see her to ask her, though I'm thinking she saw him,' her mother commented dryly. 'No, but did you not hear Donald Bhan speaking of it when we were ceilidhing at his house the other evening? Did he not say then that you and Sandy should be sure to take Cassy fishing before she goes back? And is this not the first fine evening there's been a chance of it?'

'Ach, but Donald was joking. Everyone knew that. Cassy would never want to go fishing. Certainly she didn't take the suggestion seriously because when I looked across at her she was pulling a face at the idea of it. Cassy would soon take fright if she was told to put one foot in a dinghy, never mind have anything to do with live fish.' She saw her mother's eyebrows lift sceptically. 'She's not really expecting to come with us, is she?' she asked, doubt creeping into her tone.

'Seeing you didn't warn her she couldn't come and seeing she's now seen what a handsome young man is Sandy, I do believe she's keen enough.' her mother replied. 'Maybe she's been missing all the Glasgow young men she talks so much about.' Katy smiled leniently. 'The Dear knows whether she'll be so keen once she's seen the size and state of Sandy's boat,' her mother continued. 'And so far as use goes I'm thinking she'll be no more use than a straight hook.' She shot Katy a quizzical glance. 'So Sandy knows nothing of her plan to come with you?' she asked.

Katy gave a negative shake of her head. 'How would he when I didn't know myself?' A slight frown showed between her eyes. Sandy certainly did not know and she was imagining his consternation when she turned up at the shore with her glamorous cousin all set to try her hand at fishing. 'Oh my!' she whispered under her breath, and made a grimace of dismay. There was no doubt that until this moment she been enjoying the company of her vivacious cousin but Cassy was far too dainty and squeamish to endure, let alone enjoy, the rigours of mackerel fishing from a small dinghy.

Doubtful as to the reason why her cousin had decided she wished to join them, she recalled the evening when Donald Bhan had joked about their taking Cassy fishing. The mention of it had brought hoots of ridicule, not least from Cassy herself. Now Katy chided herself on not having been more vocal in rebutting the suggestion since it seemed, if her mother's assumption was correct, that her cousin had been misled by her silence into imagining she might be welcome to join her and Sandy on one of their fishing trips. She was appalled. For them fishing, though it provided an enjoyable pastime, was a serious business since not only did it enable them to supply their own families with much-welcome fish but it also ensured Sandy being able to replenish the barrels of salt mackerel which was the essential bait for the lobster creels, which provided the greater part of his earnings.

Katy refilled her cup and went to stand in the doorway looking out at the sea. The first decent night for fishing they'd had for a couple of weeks, she reflected vexedly, and the signs were that there were plenty of mackerel there for catching. Sandy would surely be expecting to catch at least a couple of hundred fish before they either gave up or lost the shoals. He would most certainly not welcome a passenger. She hoped fervently that Cassy would change her mind about coming when she realized that mackerel fishing was likely to be no pleasure trip for her. But if she insisted then nothing could be done about it.

Unquestionably Sandy would regard Cassy as an encumbrance but, disgruntled as he might feel, Katy knew that outwardly he would accept the situation. The innate courtesy common to all islanders, which was now restraining her from withdrawing what Cassy had so mistakenly taken to be an invitation, would likewise restrain him from revealing any sign of resentment at the presence of her cousin. Stifling her self-reproach at having to inflict him with Cassy's presence, she resigned herself to hoping her cousin might be so horrified by the sight of Sandy's rough dinghy which despite lavish tarring, stubbornly continued to let in water, that she would refuse to set foot in it.

'I'm thinking Sandy won't be too pleased,' her mother ventured. 'Or maybe he's fancying a bit of Glasgow company,' she added with a whimsical smile. 'No doubt it will make a change for him.'

Katy shrugged. 'Maybe,' she agreed lightly. 'He's been that keen to keep out of her way up to now I believe he's not spoken a word to her yet.' Bending down, she took a thick homespun jersey of her father's from a box under the bench and pulled it over her head. It hung from her shoulders to her knees, enveloping her sturdy young body like a cloak. She topped it with a stiff oilskin which reached below the tops of her gumboots and finally she tied a woollen scarf over her hair. It was her regular fishing attire and proof against spray and cold.

'I hope you told Cassy to be sure and put on some suitable clothes,' she said to her mother.

'Indeed I did so,' her mother assured her. 'But will she have any suitable clothes?' she pointed out. 'I told her to take something of your father's out of the box there but she laughed at me just. We can but wait and see how she turns herself out.'

Katy was standing beside the table hurriedly gulping down the last of her tea when the door of the bedroom opened and Cassy appeared, clad in a shiny scarlet macintosh, scarlet sandals which revealed bare feet with scarlet-painted toenails, and with her blonde hair only partly concealed beneath a transparent headsquare which was tied back so as not to hide her glittering earrings. Katy

44

regarded her in wide-eyed astonishment. Her mother gave a chuckle of remonstrative laughter.

'Ach, lassie my dear, you cannot be going fishing in clothes like that. I'm saying it must be millionaires not mackerel you'll be setting out to catch this night,' she chaffed her niece.

'What's wrong with them?' Cassy demanded in mock despair. 'You told me to put on a waterproof and so I have. Goodness knows why, though,' she added, peering through the window. 'It's not raining, is it?'

'And not likely to,' Katy intervened. 'But you'll not need the rain to wet you. The sea will do that, sure enough. But you'll not only find it cold you'll very likely ruin your clothes at the same time. Sandy's dinghy's no armchair. If you're really sure you want to come fishing you'd best borrow these.' Bending down she produced a jersey similar to the one she herself was wearing. 'And these gumboots, they'll be a bitty big for you but no matter. And there's an old oilskin of my mother's which will cover you.'

It was now Cassy's turn to scream with laughter. 'Wear those things? No thank you very much,' she declined emphatically. 'I'm not going around looking like a sack of peats. I should think the sight of you in those clothes, Katy, would be enough to frighten away the fish,' she taunted, her glance deriding the shabbiness and shapelessness of Katy's attire.

Katy grinned forbearingly. 'It hasn't done so yet,' she retaliated. 'And anyway they'll keep out the wet and cold which is more than your fancy clothes will do for you. Be warned, Cassy,' she went on, 'even at this time of year it can get pretty cold on the water and you won't have a chance to enjoy yourself if you're cold.'

'I'll be warm enough,' Cassy asserted confidently. 'I've got a jersey and a cardigan under this.' She patted her macintosh. 'Anyway, I'd sooner freeze to death than wear ghastly old things like you're wearing.'

'I'm afraid you'll be more than likely to do that,' Katy replied, still proffering the jersey. 'At least take it with you in case you feel the need of it,' she coaxed.

Cassy shook her head, still smiling defiantly. 'There's no point in being lumbered with something you know you'll never wear,' she said. She studied Katy scornfully for a moment or two. 'Honestly Katy, you look a real freak in those clothes. Don't you care?'

'No more than the fish,' Katy rejoined, stowing the jersey back under the bench. 'We'd best be going now you're ready,' she urged her cousin. 'We don't want to upset Sandy by being late.' Not more than he'll be upset by the sight of you, she thought.

The track to the inlet was narrow and steep, becoming slippery with loose shingle as it neared the shore. Katy plodded easily a few paces ahead and, still feeling faintly irritated by her cousin's stubbornness about being suitably dressed, she deliberately ignored the sharp exclamations and frequent pauses which came from behind her as pebbles lodged themselves in Cassy's sandals. When they reached the shore they found Sandy leaning over his dinghy replacing floorboards.

'Is that the boat we're going in?' Cassy asked, her voice expressionless. Katy darted a quick glance at her cousin but if Cassy was feeling at all faint-hearted she seemed determined to betray no sign of it.

'It is indeed,' Katy confirmed.

'Coo-ee!' Cassy called out to Sandy. 'Coo-ee!'

Sandy straightened up and turned towards them. For a brief moment he stared blankly at Cassy.

'Coo-ee!' she called again, more confidently. 'You're going to have a nice surprise. I'm coming fishing with you and Katy,' she announced.

Katy caught the fleeting glance of anguish that crossed Sandy's features before he gave his attention to her cousin. His face and neck had already flushed a fiery red but he managed a stiff smile. 'Not in those clothes, surely?' he objected politely, and immediately bent again over his boat, seeking to hide his embarrassment.

'For goodness' sake what's wrong with my clothes? My aunt and Katy have both been criticizing them and now you're doing the same,' Cassy complained with pretended exasperation. 'What do you think is wrong with them, Sandy?' she wheedled.

Reluctantly he turned to face her. His eyes appraised her bashfully. 'Indeed there's nothing wrong with them that I can see,' he assured her earnestly. 'They're fine, but it's just that I'm meaning they're far too fancy for going fishing in, especially in an old boat like mine. You could get tar on them and spoil them altogether.'

'I think you're only saying that because you and Katy don't want me with you.' Cassy's lips formed themselves into a pout.

Sandy flashed a desperate look at Katy. 'No, no! That's not the way of it at all,' he denied. 'You're welcome enough but it's your pretty clothes I'm bothered about.'

'It's for me to worry about my clothes,' Cassy retorted. 'And if I'm enjoying myself I shan't mind getting a bit of tar on them. I'm sure you know lots of ways of getting it off.' Staring at him, she compelled his eyes to meet hers.

Katy, observing that Sandy's blushing appraisal had now been replaced by undisguised approval, was in no way perturbed. She recognized that her cousin was both pretty and beguiling and that her clothes, unsuitable though they might be, were nevertheless bewitching. It was to be expected, she reasoned, that any young man unused to the flattering attentions of young women would welcome the opportunity to respond.

But, intrigued by the increasing boldness of Cassy's manner, she looked hard at Sandy and, by degrees, the familiar image of him with his rare smile, the profusion of freckles beneath the downy cheeks, the copper-coloured hair which inexpert cutting invariably left as spiky as stalks of autumn bracken, resolved itself into the image of a handsome young man. She had never before seen anyone look at him with admiration and now, as if she herself were seeing him for the first time, she suddenly became conscious of the broadening shape of his youthful shoulders under the oilskin; the straightness of his back; the resoluteness that was beginning to firm his mouth and chin; and not least the directness of his blue eyes. She became aware of a swift surge of pride in him. Not until this moment had she thought of him as other than her close companion since childhood; her collaborator at work and in play and ultimately, because they were the only two of their generation living on the island, as her prospective husband.

The inevitability of their eventual union was recognized by them both and neither was so far aware of any desire that it should be otherwise. They were too young as yet but instinctively they knew the time would come when they would begin to speak of marriage plans. Until that time their shared devotion would lie cocooned in their minds and revealed only in those moments of swift comprehension of each other's thoughts which comes naturally to two people who know they are destined for each other.

'Did you remember to bring your new darra, Katy?' Sandy's voice cut into her thoughts.

'I did so.' Katy handed him the darra.

He inspected it cursorily. 'It looks a good enough one,' he said and tossed it into the boat. 'Ready then?' His hands were already grasping the gunwale of the dinghy, ready to haul it down into the water. Obediently Katy gripped the opposite gunwale and together they dragged it over the shingle and into the water.

'My, aren't you both strong?' enthused Cassy, picking her unsure way down behind them.

Sandy tried not to meet her adulatory glance. Instead he looked down at her feet. 'You're going to get your feet wet and spoil your pretty shoes into the bargain,' he warned her.

'We warned her ourselves. Both my mother and me,' Katy interposed with a smile. 'But she wouldn't heed us when we offered to lend her gumboots.'

Sandy silenced her with an oddly recriminatory glance. 'Indeed I don't suppose your cousin has had a pair of gumboots on her feet in all her life,' he declared testily.

Cassy smiled her approval. 'I could never get used to wearing those things, I'm sure,' she demurred.

'You'd best take off your sandals then,' Katy advised. 'Seeing you're bound to be getting your feet wet anyway.'

Cassy looked down at her feet and then coyly up at Sandy. 'You can carry me then,' she invited and held out her arms to him.

Marvelling at her cousin's coquetry, Katy wanted to giggle. But she curbed the mischievous smile that threatened to shape her lips as she saw the expression of despair which flitted across Sandy's face. This part of the shore could be observed from almost every house in the village and there would be no shortage of secret onlookers. She was certain Sandy would never risk the merciless teasing he would be forced to endure were he seen to be complying with Cassy's request. But, instead of the jocular refusal Katy was expecting him to make he sent only a swift reconnoitring glance towards the homesteads before picking up the slender Cassy in his arms and carrying her to the dinghy.

Katy hid her astonishment. Oh well, she excused him, he would be thinking since she was staying with us, he had best be kind to her. On the other hand he could be thinking that to have refused would have wasted precious fishing time.

'Goodness! You certainly are strong,' Cassy repeated.

'Ach, you weigh no more than a wee bird,' Sandy mumbled, proud of his strength yet evading the blatant admiration in her eyes. 'In you get, Katy,' he commanded and Katy, giving the stern a final push, climbed into the boat and sat beside Cassy on the middle thwart. Sandy rowed with strong, steady strokes until they were well out of the bay and on the open sea. 'You can take over now Katy,' he instructed. 'Make for the Dubh Sgeir. It should be good fishing there.'

As was expected of her when they were together Katy did as he directed, sliding into his place on the bow thwart and taking the oars while he moved to the stern.

Their movements rocked the boat a little and Cassy twittered apprehensively. When Sandy lifted the stern floorboards to get his own darra she screamed. 'There's water coming in through the bottom of the boat,' she cried.

'That's nothing,' Sandy said dismissively.

'It will do for a whiley,' Katy assured her. 'It'll stop as

soon as the wood has swelled. There's no need to be frightened by it.' She added practically, 'There's a bailer under your seat. If you want to do something about the water lift the floorboards beneath your feet and bale it out.'

Finding the bailer, Cassy began scooping out the water as if she feared they were in imminent danger of sinking. Katy and Sandy, catching each other's eyes, exchanged a faint smile.

Having sorted out the tackle, Sandy replaced the floorboards and sat down on the centre thwart beside Cassy, positioning himself so as to balance the boat and thus make rowing easier. Cassy, misinterpreting his motive, put down the bailer and moved closer to him. Though their backs were turned towards her Katy noted the startled turn of Sandy's head as he hunched away slightly. He made a gruff-sounding comment and though she could not distinguish the words she surmised he was warning Cassy to keep a safe distance away from him since he had begun to unwind his darra in readiness for fishing and the wayward hooks could be treacherous in the breeze. Cassy looked up at him, taking his warning with pouting remonstrance. He responded with a penitent grin which encouraged her to lean closer. This time he did not hunch away.

Unused to phlegmatic young men and determined to overcome Sandy's reticence, Cassy began flirting with him audaciously, and though at first Katy thought he looked ill at ease he was soon giving every appearance of enjoying her cousin's attention. Katy watched them unemotionally, though wishing at times they would include her in their bantering. But as their intimacy grew their voices lowered and she was able only to hear Sandy's low tones alternating with Cassy's frivolous laughter above the sound of the oars in the rowlocks and the rush of ripples as the boat slid through the water.

It was a good distance to the Dubh Sgeir and it was high time Sandy took over the oars, Katy acknowledged to herself but, reluctant to intrude, she continued to pull steadily at the oars until it began to seem to her that the two in front had become completely oblivious to her presence.

With a flick of surprise she saw that Cassy had taken one of Sandy's hands in hers and, pretending to read his palm, was stroking the long fingers lingeringly. A moment or so later her hand was rumpling his hair and measuring its varying lengths against one of her slim white fingers. Katy's lips tightened disapprovingly, her innate reserve jarred by what struck her as being over-sauciness on her cousin's part. But, she reminded herself, Cassy was on holiday and if this was her way of enjoying herself then she, Katy, must not criticize.

All the same she suffered a slight needling of discontent that Sandy appeared to be so engrossed by her cousin that he had failed to notice the strengthening breeze which was whipping up the wavelets and spray and requiring her to put more effort into her rowing. Normally, when it was just the two of them, he would either have taken over from her or at least have taken one oar. Her arms signified they were beginning to feel the strain but, too proud to remonstrate, she tested Sandy's reaction by resting on the oars while she took a few deep breaths.

'Ach, Katy! We're nowhere near the Dubh Sgeir yet,' he upbraided her. 'Is it tired you are already?'

The unprecedented derision in his tone stung the pride she had in her young strength. 'No, I am not then,' she denied firmly and began pulling even more strongly on the oars.

He's showing off, she thought mutinously, and assumed it was the effect Cassy was having on him that had caused him to speak to her so roughly.

The Dubh Sgeir, a wall of sheer black cliffs which rose steeply above the dark deep water was, despite its awesomeness, one of their favourite spots for fishing. As they drew nearer Katy slowed her stroke and the dinghy began to wallow in the heaving swell. Sandy, eager to test the fishing, stood up and, lowering his darra, probed the water for the shoals of mackerel they were certain they would find.

Katy was conscious of Cassy sitting rigidly, her hands gripping the thwarts, her face white, her eyes wide with dread, staring up at the sinister black cliffs where the swell was booming thunderously into the narrow chasms before it cascaded in rushing white foam back into the sea. When a curious low-flying gull clacked questioningly above their heads Cassy cried out sharply to Sandy but he, intent on raising and lowering his darra, paid her not even the scantiest attention.

She looked appealingly at Katy. 'I'm scared, Katy.' She mouthed the words rather than spoke them. 'I wish I hadn't come.'

'Wait until we start catching fish,' Katy consoled her. 'You'll be too excited to be scared then.'

Her reassurance was interrupted by a shout from Sandy. 'We're on to them, Katy! Just see and keep the boat where she is.' He hauled in the darra, on each hook of which there writhed a splendidly iridescent mackerel. 'They're big ones, Katy!' he gloated. 'Take a look at them.' Hastily he began unhooking the fish and throwing them into the bottom of the boat. 'See that, Cassy!' He shot a smug glance at her, obviously expecting her to be overjoyed by the sight. But Cassy's only reaction was to shriek in panic as the fish twisted and flapped around her ankles. Trying to lift her feet clear, she overbalanced and toppled backwards into the stern where she lay, her legs pedalling the air while she struggled, not very convincingly, to right herself. Such mishaps Katy and Sandy regarded as being part of the fun of being in small boats and Katy made little attempt to smother the peal of laughter which burst from her throat.

'Sandy!' commanded Cassy, holding up an entreating hand, 'help me!' She mustered a rueful smile which died when Sandy, without even turning to take notice of her plight, merely spared an arm to pull her roughly back on the thwart before resuming his fishing. Within seconds he was hauling in another darra full of fish.

As always, the moment the fish began to come in, excitement rippled through Katy, and her fingers itched to get at her own darra and join in. Working the oars so as to keep the boat over the shoal while at the same time ensuring it did not drift dangerously near the cliffs, she glanced at her new darra with its shining hooks and bright new feathers lying on the thwart beside her, and wondered how long it would be before Sandy allowed her to have a spell at the fishing.

There were about thirty fish in the boat but when next he hauled in his darra, on only one hook was there a fish. He lowered it again and it came up without a single fish. Again and again he tried. 'I believe we've lost the shoal, Katy,' he said ruefully. 'I'm not getting the feel of them at all.' He took a few turns of his line and tried again. He shook his head disconsolately. 'Try pulling the boat round a wee bitty,' he urged. 'Maybe we'll get back on to them.'

'Oh, surely we shall!' Katy ejaculated, disappointment so sharpening her tone that Sandy spared her a puzzled glance. 'I want to have the chance to try my new darra,' she explained.

He nodded agreement. 'We'll carry on till we do find them,' he promised her.

'Oh, no!' Cassy wailed. She was sitting sideways with her feet on the thwart so as to keep well out of the way of the fish and slime which now covered the bottom of the boat. 'Please, Sandy, can't we go back now?' she implored.

Sandy looked down at her, his expression one of shocked disbelief. 'Go back? With little more than a score or so of fish in the boat and the sea boiling with them? You can't be meaning it, surely?' he reasoned. 'We'd be mad to go back now.'

'I think you're mad to carry on,' Cassy retorted. 'Surely you've already enough fish to satisfy you for one night? And I'm cold,' she stressed. 'I didn't think it would get as cold as this.' Thinking she detected a moment of irresolution in Sandy's manner, she entreated, 'Please, Sandy, please let's go back.' She managed to slip a sob into her voice.

Katy, forbearing to tell her cousin she had only herself to blame that she was cold, listened unmoved to Cassy's plea. Of course they couldn't go back with so few fish in the boat. But she too had perceived Sandy's hesitancy and, knowing that since it was she who was responsible for Cassy's presence on the boat it was now up to her to intervene and save him from having either to disregard her cousin or submit to her whimperings and risk the subsequent teasing he would encounter were he to return with so few fish, she said firmly, 'I'm not going back until I've at least had the chance to try out my darra.' She sensed rather than heard Sandy's sigh of relief and, turning a blind eye to Cassy's look of heavy reproach, pulled the boat round as he had told her and rowed back in the direction from which they had been drifting while he again probed the sea with his darra.

The frustration of having lost the shoal when there had been the prospect of such good fishing filled their minds and, forgetting the huddled, sulky figure of Cassy, they carried on searching, commenting and suggesting until Sandy shouted triumphantly, 'We've got them, Katy! Yes and they're solid,' he added gleefully. 'Come and get started quickly before we lose them again,' he bade her and began winding in his own line in preparation for taking over the oars.

Katy felt a familiar throb of satisfaction as her lowered line quivered and seemed to come alive with fish. She unhooked them expertly and threw them on to the floor-boards.

Cassy, apparently deciding she must either participate or be ignored, said with limp enthusiasm, 'I'd like to have a go now.' Katy laughed indulgently. 'Why not?' pursued Cassy. 'Maybe it will warm me up a bit.'

'You've nothing to fish with,' Katy replied. Bending over, Cassy reached under the stern thwart where Sandy had stowed his tackle.

'You'll let me borrow your darra, won't you Sandy?' she called confidently. Gingerly she began to free the hooks.

Katy knew a moment of alarm before her mind ridiculed the idea that he might surrender his darra. Sandy had never been known to lend his precious darra to anyone. But instead of the spirited objection she expected to hear from him she saw that despite his obvious reluctance he was making no attempt to take the line from Cassy. He's daft, she thought. He deserves to lose it. As she turned back to her fishing she heard the sudden rattle of oars as Sandy leaped forward.

'No, Cassy! No!' he shouted. 'You're letting out too much line! You'll lose it altogether!'

'I shan't lose it.' Teasingly Cassy held the darra away from his reaching arm.

'Cassy!' he warned. 'Watch yourself!'

The next moment there was a stifled scream and Katy, fully occupied in unhooking a good catch, turned to see the panic-stricken Cassy cupping a hand over her chin while blood ran freely from her bottom lip in which a fish hook was embedded. Sandy, seeing the boat drifting perilously near the cliffs, dashed back to take the oars and row a safe distance away while Katy, well practised in the skill of removing fish hooks from her own flesh, secured her line around a thwart before turning to Cassy to instruct her how to remove the hook. But evidently Cassy's tragic eyes and tearful face were too appealing for Sandy to resist. To Katy's amazement he called to her to take the boat and as soon as she had done so he sat down beside Cassy and, taking her head gently under his arm, set about tenderly easing out the hook. He then took her handkerchief and after dipping it in the sea proceeded to wipe the blood from her chin.

Continuing to manoeuvre the boat away from the cliffs, Katy wondered at his unusual behaviour. Never before had she seen Sandy display such tenderness except to a sick cow that was too valuable to lose. But she found herself excusing his attentiveness to Cassy. After all they had come with the intention of catching fish and as they could not resume fishing until they had comforted Cassy it was only common sense that the hook should be removed as speedily as possible. To have waited while Cassy was instructed how to remove the hook herself might have resulted in their once more losing the shoal. She could understand his purpose well enough, she told herself, but what puzzled her was why he was allowing Cassy to continue clinging to his arm, not only impeding his movements but also preventing him from taking over the oars. She watched them with mounting irritation.

The closer booming of the swell reminded her of the

proximity of the Dubh Sgeir and she pulled away.

Sandy, having at last freed himself from Cassy's clinging arm was again stowing away his tackle in readiness, Katy assumed, to take over the oars and allow her to continue fishing. Instead he called tersely, 'We'd best go back now, Katy!'

Flabbergasted, Katy stared at him. 'Go back!' she expostulated. 'We have less than fifty fish in the boat and the sea is thick with them. Why should we be going back?' Given such a night at any other time it would be he who would insist on continuing until they had caught at least a couple of hundred. What reason was there for going back? After all, a small mishap with a fish hook was nothing to make a fuss about. It had happened countless times to one or other of them so why should he be so affected simply because it was Cassy? When might they get another evening when the sea conditions were so near perfect and the fish just asking to be caught?

The questions raced through her mind. Surely Sandy was not so touched by Cassy's tears that he would abandon such promising fishing? Surely, though he might have deluded her cousin into thinking he was truly succumbing to her flattery, he had not been genuinely captivated? She made herself reject the idea and certain that if she again voiced her objections he would yield to her wishes, she rested deliberately on the oars and stared at him defiantly, willing him to change his mind. But he refused to meet her glance and, unwinding her own line from the thwart where she had secured it, he stowed it away with his own.

'Come on, Katy! Get rowing,' he ordered irritably. 'Can you no see that your cousin's feeling the cold? See how she's shivering.' Cassy turned and nodded spiritless confirmation. Sandy took off his own oilskin and draped it around her.

Katy, swallowing her chagrin, suppressed a strong desire to protest that it was her cousin's own fault she was cold; that it had been Cassy's decision to come fishing despite all warnings; that she had scornfully refused to wear the warm clothes she had been offered. But, recalling the scene in the kitchen, she seemed to hear her mother's voice gently instilling into her the need to be ever tolerant of strangers. She sighed. Kinswoman or not Cassy must still be looked upon as a stranger. She waited a few moments to give Sandy a chance to come and take over the rowing, but making no attempt to do so he again sat down beside Cassy.

Dismay mounting at every stroke, she began to row back. She could no longer make excuses for Sandy. Indeed she was ashamed of him, she admitted to herself. Ashamed and also angry. But as her eyes rested on Cassy's slim shoulders nestling against Sandy's not unwilling arm she was conscious of some other emotion which she had hitherto not experienced. An emotion which could not be explained away by the failure of the evening's fishing nor by her displeasure with Sandy.

Back at the shore Sandy said, 'You'll stay and gut the fish, Katy?' His tone was barely interrogatory. 'It's best if Cassy doesn't hang about down here seeing she's upset and I'm thinking she'd rather I go up the brae with her.' Cassy was clinging to his arm, making it obvious she would prefer Sandy's company.

'Very well,' Katy acquiesced stiltedly. But as she gutted the fish – a task she and Sandy were accustomed to sharing – her normally smooth brow was creased by a frown of disapproval.

The fact that the brae seemed steeper and that the strings of gutted and cleaned fish seemed heavier than usual she attributed to disappointment coupled with tiredness after doing most of the rowing, but her mind was still in a turmoil when she entered the kitchen where several of the neighbours were ceilidhing with her parents. Sandy was sitting on the bench morosely drinking tea when he was not countering, with as much flippancy as he could summon, the ribald tauntings as to the reasons for their meagre catch. Cassy was sitting as close as she could get to the fire, her swollen lip emphasizing her pouting look and, Katy had to admit, enhancing her glamorousness. She appeared to be well recovered since she had plenty to say, though she repeatedly lamented that she could neither eat nor drink because of the soreness.

Katy hung up the strings of fish, shed her extra clothing and, evading her mother's searching glance and the attempts of the neighbours to include her in their badinage, poured herself a cup of tea and sat down on the fender, feigning indifference to the conversation and sporadic laughter which flowed round her.

At last Sandy rose to go. 'Oidhche mhath!' he bade them. At the door he paused. 'It looks as if it will make another fine day tomorrow,' he observed. There was a general murmur of agreement.

'Maybe the fish will be feeling that much in need of your company tomorrow they'll be fairly leaping into the boat,' one of the men jibed as Sandy stepped outside. Katy almost winced in pity for him.

'Katy,' her mother pleaded. 'If you're not feeling too tired I'm wondering will you go along to Sandy's mother and get the samples of wools from her? I'm wanting to send away some fleece tomorrow, seeing Angus says he's away to the mainland, and I'm needing the samples to choose from.'

Katy rose. 'No, I'm not tired at all,' she replied and followed Sandy into the midnight twilight that was still woven with the sound of distant gull cries and pierced by the nearer drumming of snipe. They walked together but, each sensing the uneasiness that lay between them, they exchanged only taut monosyllables until they reached Sandy's home.

'You go inside and talk to my mother,' he said, pausing by the stone dyke that bounded the garden. 'I'm staying out here for a smoke.'

She collected the knot of wool samples and lingered for a few moments talking to his mother. When she came out again Sandy was still standing by the dyke and scuffing aimlessly at the loose stones in the road. As she approached he lit another cigarette.

'Oidhche mhath!' she said as she passed him.

'Oidhche mhath!' he replied but before she had gone more than a few paces he called out to her. Obediently she retraced her steps and stood before him waiting composedly for what he wished to say.

'Katy . . .' he began haltingly, his voice roughening so he had to clear his throat before he could continue. 'Katy, I was just wanting to say to you . . .' Again he had to clear his throat. Throwing away his cigarette, he heeled it into the ground. 'See, it's this way Katy . . . It's your cousin, Cassy . . . I like her a lot. There's no doubt she's a right bonny girl . . .'

'She is indeed,' agreed Katy warmly, knowing it to be true. But she found she no longer wanted to meet his eyes and it seemed to her that something inside her which hitherto had been staunch and unassailable was slowly fragmenting and being supplanted by an ache of foreboding which deepened with every word he spoke.

'She's different . . . different from you, isn't she . . .?' Sandy continued, still fumbling for words. 'What I'm meaning is . . .' He managed a shame-faced grin and his voice strengthened with derision. 'I mean I cannot see you wearing those sort of fancy clothes, eh Katy? And not those shoes and your toenails all painted!'

She accepted his remarks with a forced chuckle. Sandy looked away quickly and then looked down at the ground between them. He began to shuffle uncomfortably as if he were still struggling for the right words. Katy waited tensely. She knew him so well; knew that he was bracing himself to tell her something and that he was ashamed of what he was going to say. The lurking ache in her stomach tightened to a pain but she made herself look up at him; made her lips shape themselves into a tranquil smile that was intended to conceal the dread she suspected showed in her eyes.

With an effort Sandy appeared to screw up his courage and at last his words came out in a rasping, stammering rush. 'You'll understand what I'm wanting to say, Katy? About how I feel about Cassy? I'm saying she's a nice girl . . .' Again he began to kick savagely at the pebbles. 'I'm not meaning to say anything that will upset you, but . . .' His tone changed to entreaty. '. . . But Katy, don't bring her out fishing with us again or I'm thinking we'll never catch any fish.'

She remained so still after he had finished speaking that he looked at her anxiously, fearing he had offended her. 'I know fine she's your cousin and you have to be nice to her,' he started to excuse himself. 'But . . .'

'It's all right, Sandy.' Her smile was genuine now and the pain inside her had given way to a leaping elation that made her want to kick off her boots and dance. 'It's all right, Sandy,' she repeated. 'I understand.'

They were looking straight at each other, their eyes reflecting mutual comprehension, and as if abashed by the extent of his relief he hurriedly lit another cigarette and drew a deep satisfied puff. 'Tomorrow night then, Katy,' he said. 'Just the two of us?'

'Tomorrow,' she promised, flicking a glance at the sky. 'If the weather holds.'

He studied the sky more critically. 'It will,' he assured her with a glad certainty. 'We'll likely fill the boat.'

'Oidhche mhath then, Sandy,' Katy said again. 'I'd best be on my way.'

'Oidhche mhath,' he bade her cheerfully.

The night was so still he could hear her retreating footsteps on the flinty road and as he entered the cottage he was vaguely aware that they had quickened as if she had broken into a run. But he had closed the door behind him and so did not hear when she began to sing.

4

Because of an Elephant

'You know, my dear, I was born because of an elephant!' the lofty memsahib voice of 'the Countess' announced immediately following her more conventional greeting, and as she settled herself into a chair facing the mirror, her faded blue eyes watched keenly for my astonished reaction. Being well practised in simulating virtually every degree of expression, I duly responded by exaggeratedly raising my eyebrows, whereupon a satisfied smile briefly puckered her lips.

Though patently of top-drawer breeding she was by no means a countess but the second wife of the old laird who once had owned the whole estate. On the laird's death his son by his first wife, having inherited the property, had promptly sold it and after seeing his stepmother settled in a suitable nursing home had evidently forgotten her existence.

The old laird's first wife had been highly regarded by the crofters on the estate but his second wife – the Countess as they had nicknamed her – was looked upon as an unwelcome intruder. I had gathered from anecdotes related by indoor and outdoor staff at the big house that she was both supercilious and autocratic. 'Claps her hands when she wants you just the same as she claps them at her little dog when it shits on the carpet,' one of the maids complained, and Tearlach, one of the ghillies, was heard to say, 'I don't know where he got her from but she has some awful queer habits.'

While the laird was alive and she was still living in the big house I had never once set eyes on the Countess and it was not until I took Morag, my old landlady, to visit her niece who was the deputy matron of the nursing home where the Countess was a resident that I eventually came into contact with her, and then it had not been preplanned. It had happened one day, after I had deposited Morag, that I had been passing through the reception hall when the Countess, catching sight of me and deciding – she always decided, never assumed – I was a visiting hairdresser, had coaxed me up to her room and had then buttonholed my attention with her startling revelation about the circumstance of her birth.

Much later I had come to wish that I had not manifested my then genuine interest since it had enouraged her to waylay me, make the same announcement, tell me the same story and expect the same reaction every time I accompanied Morag to the home. I'd soon discovered she was in the habit of greeting all her visitors similarly and alas, repetitively, the unfeigned astonishment of those hearing the story for the first time amply compensating for the scarcely concealed boredom of those who had grown overweary of the persistent recital. The reiteration had naturally resulted in the number of her visitors dwindling until finally, except for the medical staff, I had become her only caller. Despite her autocratic manner she was obviously lonely and I had continued my visits for that reason, accustoming myself to slipping into an attitude of awed attention, though letting my thoughts dwell on other things, while I brushed her hair and she recounted for the umpteenth time the dramatic circumstances which had surrounded her birth.

She had been born, she told me, in India during the heyday of the British Raj, when her father had been the highly respected tutor to the sons of an enormously wealthy maharajah. It had so happened that shortly before her birth the eldest of the princely sons had come of age and, as such an important occasion merited sumptuous celebrations, there was to be a grand procession followed by many days of feasting and rejoicing for all the maharajah's subjects. In recognition of his esteemed position in the household the Countess's father had been assigned an honoured place well in the vanguard of the procession and mounted on one of the richly caparisoned elephants, each of which was in the charge of a splendidly attired mahout.

Along the processional route there had been erected, especially for the occasion, several canopied pavilions where the more eminent guests could be assured of reasonable comfort and an excellent view of the proceedings. In one of these pavilions a seat had been reserved for the Countess's mother, who had come out to India as a young bride only twelve months previously and who by this time was seven months pregnant with the Countess. Because of her condition the more seasoned memsahibs, stressing the inescapable heat and the torment of dust and flies, had counselled the young mother-to-be to stay away from the processional route but so eager had she been to witness her dear husband's participation in such a prestigious ceremony that she had chosen to reject their advice.

As the clamorous procession had advanced the wife's eyes were focused on the elephant on which her husband was mounted and suddenly, to her horror, she saw the hitherto placid animal pick up the attendant mahout and fling him into the crowd. The next instant, carrying its helpless rider with it, the elephant was charging with wild and savage trumpetings through the scattering throng of onlookers. Heedless of the pursuit and shouted objurgations of other mahouts, the distracted animal lumbered on until it had disappeared from sight among a grove of mango trees. Convinced she would never again see her husband alive the mother-to-be had collapsed on the spot. Rushed to the nearest bungalow she had there given birth prematurely to a baby girl, born – as the Countess felt she could justifiably claim – 'because of an elephant'. The happy sequel to the day's misadventure had been that before the baby was more than an hour or two old, the ecstatic mother was being embraced by her delighted husband who, due to his resourcefulness in grasping an overhanging branch and clinging on, had escaped serious injury, or even death with no more than a few scratches.

As Morag's trips to see her niece had become regular quarterly jaunts for the pair of us so I had come to see more of the Countess. Sometimes one or other of our neighbours would join us on the pretext that he or she wanted to get something they were unable to buy from the various mail-order catalogues. More often than not it was Hector, the village philanderer, who liked to escape work whenever he could find an excuse. I was surprised to see, one day when he proposed to join us, that he was wearing his kilt and jacket rather than the somewhat shapeless homespun which was his normal attire.

'You do look smart,' I complimented him. 'Are you going somewhere special?'

'Indeed no, I am not then. I just fancied wearing my kilt.'

'Surely he's going somewhere special,' contradicted Morag teasingly. 'Isn't he going with you to visit the Countess?'

'Are you really?' I asked.

'Damty sure I'm not,' Hector denied indignantly.

'That's a pity,' I observed. 'She's very lonely these days and she would probably be glad to see you.'

'I've no doubt she would,' agreed Hector. 'But would any man in his sense go near that woman when he's wearing a kilt? Is that not right, Morag?'

'Indeed you're wise,' she confirmed.

'What's the reason for that?' I probed.

Morag explained. 'When I used to work in the kitchen of the laird's house the old laird liked to wear a kilt. And it suited him. He had a fine figure for it with his red hairy legs and a good stomach to fill it out, but then when he got this other woman for his wife he had to give up wearing it altogether.'

'She didn't like to see him wearing it?' I suggested.

'She liked it too much,' Morag repudiated. 'But every time he wore it she would go up behind him and put her hand up his kilt and squeeze his obstacles. Many's the time I'd hear him give a great shout but he couldn't stop her doing it so he just gave up wearing the kilt.'

'It wasn't just the laird she went for,' Hector pursued. 'She'd do the same to any man in a kilt. I found that out for myself. And I can tell you it hurts like hell. I believe it could have made less of a man of me too if Behag hadn't sat me in a bowl of cold water when I told her. No,' he emphasized, 'I would never go near that woman without I'd see there was a mouse trap up my kilt first.'

I was laughing so much I almost steered the car into a roadside ditch.

The subject of the Countess rarely failed to provide us with anecdotes to relate on our journeys to and from the home. Morag said her niece had described the old lady as being easily the most singular character anyone could ever recall having had in their care; that on her arrival she had immediately deluded herself into believing she was the mistress of the imposing mansion which, until its conversion to a nursing home, had been the residence of a titled and wealthy family. It had not been long before she had begun issuing imperious commands to both indoor and outdoor staff and as she had become increasingly assured of her rank there she had come to regard it as her duty to be on hand to bid departing callers, whether they were tradesmen or the relatives and friends of the other residents, a graciously condescending farewell. It seems there were many moments of comedy in observing the bewildered reactions of total strangers when they saw the Countess advancing upon them with outstretched hand while exclaiming, 'So very kind of you to call, my dear. Do come again soon, won't you?' Certainly none of the staff would ever forget the dazed expression on the face of the undertaker the first time he was bade farewell in precisely these terms.

Since Morag and the other crofters flatly refused to go within earshot of the Countess it had been left to me to observe for myself the idiosyncracies of her character. My visits had not always been an endurance test. In her room she still kept many of the relics of her exotic past, the most impressive being an intricately carved chest lavishly ornamented with brass inlay and studded with unpolished jewels. In this chest she had stored many of her most cherished mementos and sometimes, in my presence, she liked to take out one or two of them for me to admire while she narrated – I fear almost as repetitively as her usual greeting – the memories they evoked for her.

A finely chased silver casket adorned with sizeable rubies and emeralds had been one of the gifts her father had received from the Indian potentate when he had retired to the vast tea estate which his employer had earlier granted him. An ivory-handled knife, its blade and handle resplendent with gold and silver inlay, had been given him by one of his princely pupils in gratitude for saving him from a charging boar during a pig-sticking expedition. A set of small but exquisitely inlaid silver boxes had been given to the Countess herself by one of the younger princes who had been a childhood playmate. A family of ivory figures had been carved especially for her by a son of their chief house boy. The boy had been badly crippled as the result of being attacked by a tiger but with the help and encouragement of the Countess he had become a skilled craftsman. And then, looking out of place among the more glamorous items, was a plain glass whisky decanter which, at the time of the Mutiny, an uncle of hers had reckoned the only thing worth saving when he had fled into the jungle to escape the slaughterous bands of mutineers. Subsequently the decanter had become in the nature of a mascot and had been willed to the Countess on his death.

The object which I found most intriguing among all her treasures, however, was the large leather brass-studded collar which, she said, had been worn by her pet panther Narroo. She'd found the panther kitten whimpering and almost starving, beside the dead body of its mother and, taking pity on it, had carried it home to rear. Despite the terrified pleadings of the servants she had been allowed to keep the panther until it was full grown and allowed itself to be led by its collar and lead.

The Countess claimed she had absolutely no fear of any animal and that Narroo the panther obeyed her commands as willingly as any dog. She illustrated this by telling me the story of the young man who had once come to court her. It seemed that, when she had reached her early teens, her parents had decided that she needed to be weaned from the company of the children of the servants and her collection of animals and, in spite of her reluctance, introduced to the social life of the all-important Club. So, to the Club she was taken and there she had met a handsome young officer who had appeared to be much attracted to her. Her approving parents had promptly invited the young officer, along with a brother officer as companion, to a function at their home. A week or so later when the young men had been riding over to accept the invitation, they had spotted the Countess on her way, as they thought, to meet them. Unfortunately no one had warned the men of Narroo, and suddenly catching sight of her being followed by a full-grown panther they had naturally assumed she was being stalked as a kill. The accompanying officer had instantly slid from his pony and shinned up the nearest tree but the would-be-suitor, seeing the panther crouch, which it had done in obedience to a command from the Countess, had been certain it meant imminent attack and levelling his rifle he had been about to take aim when he was halted by a loud scream from the Countess. The next moment she too had crouched and had thrown her arms protectively around the panther's neck. Dumbstruck, the young officer had stood listening to her angry tirade and, having finally understood the gist of it, had hastily mounted his pony and departed, followed immediately by his treed companion. The Countess invariably ended the story with a contemptuous chuckle.

Despite her claim to have no fear of any animal her boast was, in a curious way, to be proven untrue. It had happened one day when she'd decided some of her treasures were in need of cleaning and, since she was adamant that no one should touch them but herself, she had issued instructions to the staff to bring the required polishes and cloths to her room. Unusually for such a well-run home there had at the time occurred some small contretemps which had resulted in her orders not being swiftly complied with, and becoming increasingly exacerbated by the delay the old lady had made her own way to the cleaning room. There she had collected the necessary polishes and, spotting a pile of clean dusters only fractionally above her reach, she had dragged out a suitable box on which she could stand. The box was low and sturdy and one would have thought there could be little risk of an accident but, just as she had been about to grasp a bundle of dusters, a mouse had sped suddenly over the back of her hand. Poor Countess! To her, panthers and other animals of the jungle may have been 'cuddlies', but the sudden appearance of the tiny mouse had unnerved her to such an extent that, jerking back, she had hit her head on the bracket of a shelf behind her and, stumbling off the box, had fallen heavily on her side, losing consciousness as she did so.

As soon as she had been missed the search had begun but since none of the staff could conceive for one moment the idea that the dignified Countess might ever have allowed herself to penetrate the housemaids' quarters, the small cleaning room was among the last places to be investigated. As a consequence she had been lying there for some time before she had been discovered. Hospital examination revealed she had concussion and a fractured hip.

She was old and frail and she slipped away so quickly that it was only a little over a week before the undertaker had accepted her final invitation to 'Be sure and call again very soon, won't you?'

Despite her often exacting behaviour she was sincerely mourned by everyone connected with the home, the staff admitting to feeling as bereft at her passing as if she had indeed been a revered chatelaine.

I remember her with affection and amusement and at times like to imagine her arrival at the pearly gates. Did she, when confronted by St Peter, announce in that distinctive memsahib voice of hers: 'You know, my dear, I was born because of an elephant'? And then I confess my imagination runs on and I wonder . . . Ah, yes, I do dare to wonder if some minor angel whispered in a puckish aside to St Peter, 'Maybe she was born because of an elephant but she died because of a tiny wee mouse!'

5

The Distant Loving

With only two days to go before the end of the term and only minutes before the gong would be sounding for the end of the afternoon's lessons, Miss Melly's pupils were giving their atlases the restless inattention which regularly afflicted them once exams were over and the long summer vacation approached. Simply as a means of focusing their attention she had set them the undemanding task of refreshing their knowledge of the location of harbours and fishing ports around the British Isles.

'Please, Miss, which of these little islands in the Hebrides is the one where you spend your summer holidays?' one of the girls asked.

There was a general titter of amusement. The girl had pronounced the word 'He-brides', but Miss Melly, knowing the mispronunciation had been deliberate so as to create a small diversion, nevertheless corrected the girl without remonstrance. She too was bored with harbours and fishing ports. Bored too with teaching. It had been her parents who had insisted on her entering the teaching profession and she had never had the spirit to oppose them. Beckoning the girl to bring the atlas to her, she circled the island with her pencil before sending her back to her desk.

'Gosh! It's tiny! Look!' the girl exclaimed, displaying the atlas to the other pupils who were craning their necks to see.

'Is there much to do there, Miss?' another girl asked.

'I find plenty to do.'

'What sort of things, Miss?'

'Well, I go birdwatching and sealwatching and sometimes I see porpoises and sharks. And I search for wild flowers to add to my collection and I roam the rocky parts of the shore looking for fossils. I find it absorbingly interesting.'

'Is that all though, Miss? I mean isn't there anything exciting to do?'

'What do you call exciting?'

'Well, dances and concerts and things,' the girl said.

'Oh, absolutely nothing like that,' Miss Melly smiled. 'But there's nothing so exciting as going fishing, especially so when you get a good catch. And then it's exciting to help the crofters gather in their harvests when it's a rush to rescue it before it's drenched by the storms. It's all done by hand you see, just as it's been done for hundreds of years.' She paused and then seeing the girls were willing her to continue, not so much because the topic interested them but because it saved them studying their atlases, she resumed, 'Being on a tiny island gives one an enormous sense of freedom and independence. I can trudge the moors and hills or I can laze around. I can go fishing in a rowing boat or I can just sit by the shore and fish. Everything I do depends either on the weather or my mood.' Her mood at that moment switched rapidly from tolerance to impatience for the gong to sound. She wanted to forestall further questions about the island. Already the subject was threatening to evoke too many memories.

'Shall you be going there again this summer, Miss?'

Miss Melly winced. Surely, surely the gong was late? She cleared her throat so as to account for the lurking break in her voice. 'No, as a matter of fact I'm planning to go somewhere quite different this year. A more sophisticated place perhaps.'

'Oh, do tell us where, Miss.'

'No,' she said, and trying to ward off further questions she invited, 'You tell me where you're all going.'

Mercifully at that moment the gong sounded a reprieve and the classroom became instantly noisy with the shuffling of feet and the banging of desks. There was a random chorus of 'Good afternoon, Miss', as the girls scurried out of the room to race along the corridor towards their lockers. As their voices died away Miss Melly got up from her desk and resignedly closed the door behind them. She should, she knew, have insisted on the last pupil to leave returning

70

to close the door but she'd always been an indifferent disciplinarian and on this particular afternoon she felt disinclined to utter reprimands. Putting away her own books she closed her desk, but instead of locking it and leaving the room as she normally did she sat down again and taking off her thick-lensed spectacles she leaned her elbows on the top and stared out of the window, seeing only hazily the distant white-clad figures already making their way towards the tennis courts.

She had not foreseen the interest her pupils might have in the island where, for the past ten years, she had been accustomed to spending the whole of her summer vacation, and their artless questioning had touched a still-exposed nerve, triggering off the lingering sorrow which, for the past year, she had been trying to expunge from her mind. As the school settled into its afternoon abandonment her resolve weakened and she began yet again to rake over the debris of her once-cherished memories.

She vividly recalled the advertisement in a magazine through which she had been browsing – an advertisement which, she had later convinced herself, fate had destined her to see and respond to . . .

'Clean, comfortable accommodation in summer for one or two ladies in crofter's cottage in the Hebrides,' the advertisement offered, and on an impulse she jotted down the name and address of the advertiser.

She had, for some time, been telling herself she would like a break from the regular continental holidays which she and Miss Boyd, the deputy headmistress, had been taking together for the past four or five years. It was not that she had not enjoyed their holidays – Miss Boyd being a capable organizer and also an excellent linguist had always ensured everything had gone according to plan – but not only was Miss Boyd some years older than herself but she was averse to even the smallest leaning towards unconventionality, a taste which Miss Melly had sometimes imagined she herself would enjoy. Increasingly of late she had become aware of a slight tingle of mutiny against the recurrent unadventur-

71

ousness of their holidays, but her own suggestions had brought only reproaches and criticism from Miss Boyd and as each holiday was proposed she had submitted meekly to her companion's plans.

But now, on the page in front of her a chance offered itself. Why did they not try the Hebrides for their next holiday? It was not a foreign country so there would be no language difficulty. And at least a holiday there would be different from their usual sightseeing, swimming and basking in the sun. Without further hesitation Miss Melly wrote asking for more information, and when the reply arrived, signed by a 'Mrs Marjac Macfee (widow)', she decided that wherever Miss Boyd might choose to spend her next holiday she herself was going to insist on sampling a stay in the widow Marjac Macfee's Hebridean cottage.

As Miss Melly expected, Miss Boyd was aghast at the proposal. 'It's so bleak and isolated up there,' she objected with a shudder of distaste, but Miss Melly stayed unusually resolute and in the end it was Miss Boyd who gave in. 'I think you're being very foolish,' she chided. 'But seeing you intend to be obstinate about it I may as well come with you and try to save you from any further folly.'

Miss Melly had been nursing a secret hope that Miss Boyd would flatly refuse to accompany her but as the time for the holiday drew nearer her innate timidity reasserted itself and she admitted to herself that she was by no means reluctant to have a companion.

The widow Marjac had written giving them instructions as to how to proceed once they had left the train. They should make for the pier, she told them, and there they would find the 'big' ferryboat which would take them to the island. She had given word to the skipper of the ferry that she was expecting them so he would be keeping a look-out for them. When they reached the island she herself would be waiting to meet them. It all sounded quite simple and straightforward. It turned out not to be so.

The long train journey had been tiring but it had offered the recompense of changing views lit by sunshine and cloud shadows. Arrived at the terminus, however, they were met

72

by a low-hanging mist which had totally obscured the land and seascape and thoroughly dampened their thin summer clothes before they reached the pier. And there they found no ferryboat waiting. Used to continental-type ferries, they had been expecting a vessel of similar size, and during the train journey when they had murmured against the stuffiness of their compartment they had comforted each other with the prospect of a wind-cooled stroll around the deck of the boat, and hopefully a long cool drink from the bar. Disillusionment came when a man in oilskins approached them and after inquiring brusquely if they were for 'Mistress Macfee' led them to a boat which looked to them as being no more accommodating than the most basic canal cruiser. There was no deck to promenade and the cabin was simply a space beneath the foredeck, along each side of which slatted wooden seats appeared to be the only concession to comfort.

Miss Boyd treated Miss Melly to an expostulatory glance before her lips tightened in unspoken accusation. Miss Melly, struggling to make light of the situation, summoned her most autocratic voice and confronted the skipper.

'We were given to understand it was to be the big ferryboat which would be taking us to the island,' she challenged him.

'Aye, right enough. This is the big ferryboat. The small one's overby.'

For a few moments they stood hesitantly on the pier, Miss Melly half expecting her companion to refuse to board the boat.

'Are you two ladies coming aboard?' the skipper called peremptorily.

'It's a calm day,' Miss Melly encouraged Miss Boyd, who was no sailor.

In the limited shelter of the forepeak they sat side by side on the wooden seats, Miss Boyd too angry and too fearful of being so close to the water, Miss Melly too crestfallen to be in any mood for conversation, while both were wishing desperately that visibility would improve sufficiently to give them something to look at other than each other and the grey surround of sea now pitted with spiritless rain-drops.

When, after about an hour the steadily throbbing engine slowed, two shrill blasts on the ferry's siren pierced the silence and then from across the water there came a shout which was answered by the skipper. The exchange was followed by the steady sound of oars in rowlocks and out of the greyness a small dinghy emerged and came alongside the ferry. Immediately one of the two ferrymen seized their suitcases and lowered them into the waiting arms of the oarsman.

'What are you doing with our luggage?' Miss Boyd demanded as if she suspected piracy.

'Surely it is the Mistress Macfee's place you are wanting?' the ferryman countered. 'Now if you'll step to the rail just I will hand you down to the boatman who will row you ashore.'

Miss Boyd's mouth opened in consternation. 'I am not getting down into that little boat!'

'There is no other way you will get ashore, Madam,' the man reasoned.

Miss Boyd turned on Miss Melly with her 'look at what you've let us in for' expression, but Miss Melly, though petrified at the thought of getting into the unsteady dinghy, had already launched herself at the man's arm and was in the process of being handed down, just as their luggage had been, into the ready grasp of the oarsman who, with the lack of gallantry she had learned to expect from men, pushed her unceremoniously down on to the thwart. Miss Boyd, still vehemently opposed to the idea but realizing she was separated from her luggage and from her companion, hung back for only a few tense seconds before she allowed herself to be similarly treated. 'I'm going straight back to the mainland as soon as I've had a night's sleep,' she hissed in Miss Melly's ear as she collapsed on the thwart beside her.

The widow Marjac was waiting for them as she had promised, and immediately Miss Melly's misgivings over her choice of holiday venue subsided. Even Miss Boyd's ill humour mellowed under the influence of the warmth of their landlady's welcome. They had been expecting her to be elderly, and certainly the stocky figure – wearing a woollen shawl over her head, a thick homespun skirt and sturdy boots – who met them on the jetty had at first sight given the impression of one belonging to an earlier generation than themselves. In her cottage and without her shawl she appeared to be little more than middle-aged. Her gait was still lithe; her thick, black hair, plaited and pinned into a snood-enclosed bun, showed no trace of grey; and her skin, no doubt tautened and sheened by wind and rain, was etched only with fan-shaped laughter lines at the corners of her shrewd grey eyes.

After their meal, instead of retiring to the room the widow had indicated was to be their sitting room, they chose to linger in the kitchen, absorbed by her conversation and lilting Highland accent. Suddenly they heard from the half open door a long shrill whistle.

'That will be Euan our postman, just,' Marjac told them in answer to their glances of inquiry, and immediately swung the kettle over the fire.

'A postman? At this time of night?' Miss Melly queried, looking at her watch.

'Ach, it is about his usual time,' Marjac replied. Her words were very soon followed by slow footsteps on the cobbled path; the door was pushed wide and with a breezy greeting a tall, well-built, middle-aged man, his regulation cap and uniform lustred by mist stepped into the kitchen. And, at the same time, into the pattern of Miss Melly's life.

Marjac gave him a Gaelic greeting and then, in English, introduced them as 'my two ladies from England'.

'Oh my! And what weather this is to welcome you to our island,' Euan sympathized, coming forward to give them each a bashful but nevertheless enthusiastic handshake. 'But see now, I believe I have mail here for one of you two ladies.' Delving into his scantily filled mail bag he produced a sprawlingly handwritten letter and, squinting a little in the poor light, began reading out the name: 'Mistress Tsee-Tee-fora Melly,' he stumbled. 'Would that be the name now?'

'Theodora,' Miss Melly corrected him in precisely the same tone as she might have corrected one of her pupils, and turning to Miss Boyd she commented, 'It's sure to be from my Aunt Jessie. She always tries to jump the gun as soon as she knows the address I'm bound for.' As she stepped forward to claim the envelope from Euan his fingers touched hers – she thought not accidentally – and glancing up at him in surprise she noticed the quick flush that had risen to his cheeks. Not divining that the flush was the result of embarrassment at having had difficulty in getting his Gaelic tongue around the pronunciation of her unfamiliar English name, she naively wondered if it could have been reaction to their brief contact. The startling possibility made her blink and catch her breath.

Gawkily thin, with short, wiry, black hair and button-black eyes that appeared to bore through her thick-lensed spectacles, Miss Melly had never had any illusions about her attractiveness to men. Her mother had ensured that. 'You'll need to earn your living because with your looks no man will want to keep you,' she taunted, and since no man had ever tried, even briefly, to exert his charm on her Miss Melly had accepted that her mother had been right. Now the sudden revelation that her touch had caused a man to blush slightly unnerved her. A wild suspicion that Euan was interested in her as a woman thrust itself into her mind. Could such a thing at last have happened to her?

Lying in bed that night she let herself reflect on the likelihood of such a thing. She had never experienced any kind of romance – not even a holiday flirtation – and the possibility excited her. Why not now? her thoughts urged her. She was only in her middle thirties so she was not too old to enjoy the prospect. And no doubt Euan had never had much opportunity to meet women other than those living on the island.

Discreetly she sought to learn more about him and discovered that he was a bachelor; that he lived with his ageing mother and a younger brother who suffered from epilepsy and that his home lay just beyond the hill they could see from Marjac's cottage. In addition to being the island's postman he worked his croft, kept cattle and sheep, and also owned a motor boat which he and his brother regularly used for fishing and working lobster creels. Miss Melly soon found herself listening eagerly for the sound of the postman's whistle in the evenings.

The weather during her and Miss Boyd's stay remained wet and windy. Miss Boyd grew daily more resentful, inveighing constantly against the necessity of drying out their clothes and footwear every evening or, alternatively, of being confined to the cottage. For her, their return to the mainland could not come quickly enough. Miss Melly, though she too had been bitterly disappointed by the weather, was not the least bit impatient to leave the island. Thinking she'd noticed increasing signs of Euan's interest in her and recognizing her growing attachment to him, she ignored her companion's complaints and mentally listed the more suitable clothes she would require for her next visit.

'Surely you're not planning to go there again?' Miss Boyd upbraided her when after the turn of the year the venue of their next holiday came up for discussion.

'Certainly I'm going there again,' Miss Melly affirmed. 'I found it fascinating and I'm really keen to explore it more thoroughly.'

'Humph!' Miss Boyd jerked dismissively. 'You'll be going on your own then.'

Miss Melly experienced a swift surge of relief at the ultimatum.

The second boat trip to the island was far less daunting than the previous one. The weather was sunny; the skipper and crew were less surly and the transfer from ferry to dinghy slightly less intimidating.

As before, Marjac was waiting to greet her and in the evening after his usual whistle to announce his imminent arrival Euan also welcomed her.

'So your friend, Miss Boyd, is not with you,' Euan commented.

'No, she likes to be sure of sun when she goes on holiday and there wasn't much of that when we were here last year.'

'But you have come back in spite of the weather you had? You must have a fondness for the island?' He regarded her with warm approval.

'Certainly I want to see more of it,' Miss Melly agreed.

'It is indeed a beautiful island and I could show you places here the few tourists who have been here have never seen and are unlikely ever to see.'

'Surely there's no man loves this island so much as Euan,' Marjac interposed. 'In every kind of weather and in every season of the year he walks it from end to end, over the hills and down into the glens, and yet he's never tired of praising it. You would think it was Euan and not the Dear Lord who created it.'

'I wish you'd tell me how to get to some of these secret places,' Miss Melly said.

'I couldn't do that. Some of them could be dangerous for a stranger to go alone.'

'You must get Euan to take you on a day when he is not busy,' Marjac proposed. 'You will do that for her, will you not, Euan?'

'Aye, maybe so,' Euan agreed.

Miss Melly's hopes had been soaring during this conversation. Euan himself seemed to come as close as his shyness permitted to inviting her company. When Marjac made her proposal that she should ask him to take her she convinced herself that his interest in her was so apparent that her landlady had discerned it and had chosen this way of trying to nudge him out of his shyness. Euan's reply made her heart leap.

Interpreting his 'maybe so' as a commitment, she daily anticipated his offer to escort her to some remote part of the island. But as the weeks of her holiday went by without his referring to the project, anticipation was swamped by disappointment. She pondered whether he had been too self-conscious to voice the invitation: whether she had been too diffident in not mentioning it. It was not until the eve of her departure for the mainland at the end of her holiday that she brought herself to observe, regretfully, to Marjac that Euan had not followed up his plan to show her some of the secret places on the island. 'Was he too shy, d'you think?' she asked Marjac.

For a moment Marjac stared at her absently. 'Oh my!' she then recalled with a rueful chuckle. 'Indeed I do remember him saying that to you. Ach but that's Euan. He's one that will never say no if one asks something of him, whether or not he means it.'

Marjac's airy dismissal of Euan's behaviour hurt Miss Melly. She had been letting herself imagine that he would have been looking forward as keenly as herself to their expedition. Had he never meant to take her? Had she been deceiving herself about his interest in her? Even after she returned home the questions continued to tease her mind until she chided herself into a resolve to banish all thoughts of him until she should see him again. But she knew she had to see him again. She must know for certain whether she had been foolish to imagine she attracted him. Doubt made her restless, and long in advance of her next holiday she was as impatient to see Euan again as if there had been some pledge between them.

The shine of welcome in his eyes when they met again and his strong, lingering handshake dispelled doubts as to their mutual attraction, and smiling up at him Miss Melly felt the first quiverings of an emotion that had convinced her this was no holiday romance. She began to reflect on what might be its eventual outcome. She decided to ask Marjac to initiate her into the work of the croft and though Marjac mocked politely at the idea of an English schoolteacher working on a croft she taught her how to milk cows and feed calves; to weed potatoes and to help harvest the hay and corn.

'My but she's a hardy right enough,' Marjac enthused to Euan one evening. 'Likely she'll want to become a crofter herself one of these days,' she quipped, giving a sidelong glance at the black velvet dress and rope of pearls Miss Melly liked to wear once the outside work was over.

'You could be right,' Miss Melly agreed, glancing covertly at Euan to see his reaction.

'I believe Miss Melly's clever enough to do anything,' he said.

Working alongside each other on the croft she and Marjac had, despite their different upbringings and environment, steadily overcome much of their reserve. It resulted in their joining the ceilidhs in the ever-welcoming houses of the other islanders, and when there was no ceilidh to tempt them out or the weather confined them indoors, they shared the kitchen, Miss Melly sitting at the table sorting and labelling the various specimens she had collected while at the same time keeping her ears pricked for the sound of the postman's whistle while Marjac, occupying her usual place beside the window, busied herself with her knitting.

In response to Marjac's coaxing Miss Melly recounted stories of her student days or events which had occurred during her foreign travels with Miss Boyd. In her turn Marjac described her childhood and youth on the croft; her parents; her marriage and her subsequent widowhood after only three years. She spoke proudly of her son who was an engineer in Glasgow and whom she saw only when he came home to spend New Year with his kinsfolk on the island. At such times their understanding of each other seemed profound and yet, beneath the flow of chatter and reminiscence, Miss Melly was sometimes aware of a puzzling restraint between them. Suspecting that one of its causes might be the deference of landlady to guest, she tried to persuade Marjac to call her by her first name instead of always addressing her formally as 'Miss Melly'.

'Oh but that wouldn't be so easy,' Marjac demurred and, seeing Miss Melly's surprised eyebrows, apologized. 'It's not a name I've heard of in my life before and my Gaelic tongue would likely have trouble saying it just as Euan had.'

'Just call me Theo,' Miss Melly urged, and as Marjac appeared about to protest she stressed, 'Really and truly I'd like everyone to call me Theo. I wish you'd tell them all. It would help me not to feel such a stranger among you.'

Marjac looked troubled. 'But,' she began and then as if she'd had second thoughts about what she had been going to say she paused.

'But,' Miss Melly prodded.

'Ach, folks here would not be wanting to call you by that name.'

'Why ever not? Just because I'm English?'

'Not because you are English just,' Marjac denied. 'But you are different from us. We have great respect for you and for your learning. We would not consider we were treating you with respect if we were to call you anything but Miss Melly.'

'But I don't want respect from you. I just want to be one of you. Can't you see me as just being that?'

Marjac shrugged her shoulders and smiled at her leniently. 'Ach, if only you had the Gaelic I'd be able to explain it to you better,' she said.

She had much the same reaction from Euan when she suggested to him that he should call her by her first name. 'I would be needing to loosen up my tongue with a poultice before I could say it properly,' he joked.

'But you and Marjac are my friends and yet you are making a stranger of me,' she argued.

'You had best learn the Gaelic,' he advised. 'Folks would find it easier to talk to you if you had their language.'

She accepted his advice with alacrity. Being able to converse in their own language would certainly ease communication between her and the islanders and, since Euan was reputed to be the best Gaelic scholar thereabouts, it would give her the opportunity to persuade him to be her tutor. With this purpose in mind she made a habit, on fine evenings, of taking leisurely strolls, planning her route so as to meet up with him on his postal round and then, with the excuse of wanting to practise her Gaelic, accompany him until they reached the vicinity of Marjac's cottage.

Her decision to learn the language pleased him greatly and as summer holidays had come and gone and her knowledge of the Gaelic had increased there developed between them a jocular, easygoing relationship which she came to envisage as being the precursor to a much closer understanding between them. She yearned for his love, not with passion but with a steadfast desire to be needed and to be cared for by him. And yet she had to admit not so much disappointment as dissatisfaction that he had never even hinted at such an emotion; had never attempted to embrace her; had never even addressed her other than as Miss Melly.

She comforted herself in recalling how, much earlier in her acquaintanceship with Marjac, her landlady had retorted quite sharply when she had commented on the noticeable aloofness between the male and female populations of the island. 'We don't hold with sloppy behaviour,' she said. 'Our men would be ashamed to show their feelings. A woman soon gets to know if a man has a fancy for her and then it's for her to give him a lead.' Thus, unwittingly, Marjac had explained Euan's restraint.

Wondering if Euan expected her to 'give him a lead', she dared to tease him about his bachelorhood.

'Aye, right enough, I believe a wife could be kind of useful to me,' he confessed. 'But how would I be thinking of taking a wife when I have my old mother and my brother to look after in a house with two bedrooms only?' he demanded with a philosophical shrug of his shoulders. But his old mother was frail and couldn't live for ever, Miss Melly reflected. And then what . . .? There were times when she felt so close to him she was sure she knew. She even reached the stage of making a sketch of his cottage and kept it in her desk at school, handy so as to make notes as ideas came to improve it.

At one time she become so frustrated at being able to see Euan only in the summer, she proposed to Marjac that she could perhaps take a second holiday some time during the Christmas period. But Marjac showed no enthusiasm for having a guest in her home during the wild wet days of winter and, there being no other accommodation, Miss Melly had to forgo her scheme. The alternative was to ask Marjac to write to her and keep her informed of what was happening on the island but Marjac scoffed at the idea.

'My English is good enough only to say what I wish to say to you. It is not good enough to put it into writing. No doubt you will find my letters comical.'

'But the letter you wrote in reply to mine when I

answered your advertisement was exemplary,' Miss Melly pointed out.

'Ach, but that was Chrissie, the postmistress,' Marjac admitted. 'Chrissie is a better scholar than myself and good at writing the English.'

It was Chrissie the postmistress who subsequently acknowledged the parcels of goodies which she sent to Marjac. The acknowledgements frequently took a long time to arrive and were invariably stilted notes saying 'Marjac says to thank you for your kindness. She hopes you are well.' When she became more friendly with Euan she sent him similar parcels. It had not surprised her that they were not acknowledged, not even via the postmistress. He'd once told her he didn't often get to writing letters because his fingers had grown so stiff and bent with hauling lobster creels and baiting lines he found it difficult to hold a pen, and she knew he'd be far too shy to ask the postmistress to write on his behalf. However, he was always so appreciative when next they met she was happy to leave it that way.

Ten years rolled by and there was virtually no change in Miss Melly's life. Every summer she returned eagerly to the island, still cherishing her love for Euan; still dreaming of the time when his old mother would at last relinquish her fragile hold on life and leave him free to take a wife. And then, on a day when the spring term was drawing to its close and she was able to think of little but the prospect of seeing Euan again, there arrived a letter addressed in the postmistress's handwriting. She had no sense of foreboding, and assuming it to be the usual stilted acknowledgement of the last parcel she'd sent to Marjac, she left it unopened until her return from school.

The day had been fraught with mishaps of one kind or another and when she reached home she discovered to her dismay that the kitchen was flooded because of a burst pipe. By the time she'd finished mopping up she was more than ready for her bed and was thankful that the next day was a Saturday and there would be no school. She had already changed into her nightdress before she remembered the letter. As she had expected it began 'Marjac says I am . . .' but it did not continue that way. As she read on her hands began to shake, her throat tightened until she had almost to gasp for breath.

Collapsing into a chair, she stared incredulously at the words the postmistress had written: 'Marjac says I am to ask you what you wish her to do with the parcel you sent to Euan since there is no one now to take delivery. His old mother died a few days only before your parcel arrived. Poor soul, she grieved so much over the tragic death of her two sons last New Year she had no wish to live and now she is buried along with them. It has been a sad time for the island. Euan was always so well thought of and such a fine, upright man as you will remember. Now the empty cottage is a daily reminder to us all of the dreadful accident. If there is nothing perishable in the parcel Marjac says she will keep it until you come again.'

Again and again Miss Melly read the letter, desperately trying to convince herself that it couldn't be true; that she must have misread it; that it was not her Euan who had died but another man of the same name. When there ceased to be any room for doubt she threw herself on the bed, devastated by grief.

She wakened to find her wretchedness intensified by the bitter knowledge that not only was Euan dead but this casual and callous note was her only intimation of his death. Yet again she read the letter. 'Last New Year,' Chrissie had written. Euan had been dead for nearly three months! It was unthinkable that she'd remained in ignorance until now! Had it not occurred even to Marjac that the bereavement was as much hers as theirs? That she would have wanted to share their sadness? That she had the right to do so? After all these years when they had been so kind and welcoming that she thought of herself as being one of them had they in effect continued to look upon her as still a stranger? So much a stranger that their instinct was to exclude her from the intimacy of their mourning? A sense of rejection strengthened her resentment against them.

Hadn't they seen with their own eyes the affection between her and Euan? And yet they hadn't told her! They hadn't told her! The torturous thought beat relentlessly at her mind, and outrage at their neglect made her want to scream her condemnation into the silence of the empty flat.

Driven by the need to confirm the fact of Euan's death and desperate for knowledge of the circumstances which surrounded it, she did not cancel her holiday. Marjac was waiting on the pier to meet her but Miss Melly was too overwrought to mention Euan until after supper, when they would have been expecting to hear his whistle shrilling to announce his coming. Miss Melly forced herself to remark, 'I was shocked to hear of Euan's death.'

Marjac became grave. 'It was a terrible shock to everyone. I couldn't believe it for a long time. Not until they brought the bodies ashore.'

'What happened?' Miss Melly choked on the question.

'Weren't Euan and his brother out in their boat and hauling the creels?' Marjac enlightened her. 'It wasn't such a wild day at all but when Ally Beag was coming home from the hill he saw the two men standing up in the boat with Euan at the tiller. His brother was hauling when suddenly he seemed to fall forward into the water. Next he sees Euan go into the water and then they both disappeared and the boat was left drifting. Ally ran as fast as he could to put down his own boat and go out to them to give them a hand but there was no sign of either Euan or his brother.'

Miss Melly tried to hold back her tears. 'What do they think happened?' she asked.

'Ach, well you know Euan's brother was epileptic and folks think he must have had a fit while he was hauling and fallen overboard. Euan would surely have gone in after him but the Dear knows what came of it. Neither of them could swim and maybe one of them tangled in the rope.' She shook her head sadly and her own voice faltered into a sob as she lifted her apron to her eyes. 'You'd have thought the island had been hit by a thunderbolt with the news of it. Not a soul could believe such a thing had happened, Euan being such a fine man and strong with it. There never was such grief that I can remember.'

'I'm hurt that you never let me know about Euan's death,' Miss Melly reproached her. 'I was so fond of him and yet I heard not a word of it until Chrissie wrote to ask me what you should do with the parcel I'd sent him.'

Marjac showed little trace of repentance. 'But we got word to all who needed to know,' she reasoned. 'All his relatives, though most of them he'd not set eyes on for many a year.'

'But not to me! If I'd known I would have come for his funeral. I would have wanted my flowers to be on his grave.'

Marjac regarded her curiously. 'Why would you have wanted to come all that way just for a funeral, Miss Melly?' and when Miss Melly made no reply she resumed, 'Our island funerals are not made so much of as is the English way. Our mourning is deep and heartfelt and needs no flowers to express our sadness. And there would have been no place for you at Euan's burial; no place for you nor me nor any woman; not even the women who are kinsfolk would be at an island burial.'

Miss Melly's control broke. 'I would have wanted to say goodbye to him. To shed my tears over his body. I would have had at least that measure of relief,' she moaned pitifully. 'I'd grown to love him. There was an understanding between us.'

Marjac looked faintly embarrassed. 'But you saw him for no more than a few weeks in the year. It could only have been a distant loving,' she said bluntly.

'We saw a great deal of each other when I was here. You don't seem to understand how much Euan looked forward to my company. He told me that many times.'

'I have no doubt of it,' Marjac agreed. 'It is true enough Euan liked your company but it would be truer to say Euan liked company – any company. His post round was a long and often lonely one so it was only to be expected he would welcome anyone who was willing to help the time pass more easily.'

'But it wasn't just that,' Miss Melly was stung into

protesting. 'We'd become so close to each other, Euan and I. Oh, I know he couldn't speak of being married while his mother was alive but . . .' Her voice trailed off into a whisper.

Marjac sat down opposite her, compelling her attention. 'Miss Melly,' she began in a voice gentle with concern. 'You must try to understand what I am going to say to you. Folks knew of your feeling and your hopes for Euan. Indeed it was plain enough for all to see and it was often spoken of at the ceilidhs. They knew well it was Euan who brought you back here year after year. They thought you foolish but since you had chosen to be so and it made you happy they had no blame for Euan that he did not discourage you. You gave him your company; you sent him parcels of cigarettes and biscuits which he enjoyed. Why should you not each get some happiness out of it? That was the way they looked at it. That was the way Euan also saw it so he never minded their teasing him about you.'

Miss Melly was stricken with aversion. 'Are you telling me that people mocked Euan about his friendship with me?'

Marjac's confirmatory nod made her feel debased. So her feeling for Euan had been a subject for joking at the ceilidhs! She could almost hear their banter. To them her obvious devotion had been no more than an annual entertainment at which they had been spectators. She shuddered with mortification. 'I'd never have thought they could be so cruel,' she murmured.

'They meant no harm.' Marjac was quick to defend them. 'They have always respected you. It was just the way you looked on Euan that amused them. You didn't seem to know that the way he treated you was just part of the great respect he had for you. You didn't seem to know either that because you were not one of us Euan would never have thought of taking you for his wife.'

Miss Melly's desolation increased with every word Marjac spoke. 'Respect! Respect wasn't what I wanted. Certainly not from Euan.'

Marjac set about brewing a pot of tea. 'There now,' she

comforted, handing a cup to Miss Melly. 'Drink that and then maybe a wee dram and by the morning surely you'll not be taking things so much to heart.'

The whisky numbed her torment but when she wakened next morning her body still ached with silent weeping. She wanted to sleep on and on but was fearful of dreaming. No more dreams, she prayed. Even daydreams were too disturbing. She vowed to be more ruthless with her thoughts.

Unwilling to face the solicitous Marjac, she waited until she heard her going to milk the cows before she rose and dressed herself in readiness to roam the moors as she had done so often in the past. It was not specimens for her collection she was seeking but solace for her lacerated feelings. She did not find it. The presence of Euan was too intrusive, stirring the turmoil of her mind until her resistance weakened and she spent much of the time sitting and staring in a trancelike way at the sea which in taking him had denied her ever knowing his true feelings for her.

Returning to the cottage later in the evening she was overtaken by the new postman, a sturdy young man whom Marjac described as being always in such a hurry to finish his round that he galloped and leapt from cottage to cottage, often to the detriment of the mails which jostled in his bag. Unlike Euan he had no time to take a strupak with anyone so had no use for a whistle with which to warn of his coming. As he passed her he threw her a quick greeting and, obviously determined he was not going to allow her to delay him, rushed ahead. For her the moment was a poignant one and she needed a little time to regain control of herself before continuing on her way.

A few evenings later when she and Marjac were sharing the kitchen Miss Melly overcame her reluctance sufficiently to ask, 'Marjac, what will happen to Euan's cottage now? Will it just be left empty like so many others here? Or has he a relative to inherit?'

Marjac did not look up from her knitting and for a moment Miss Melly suspected she thought her question not to be in good taste. She was about to apologize when Marjac said stiffly, 'Euan's own son will inherit it, naturally.'

'Euan's son?' Miss Melly repeated, her voice sharp with dismay. 'Euan has a son? No one has ever mentioned that! How long ago was it?' She dreaded the reply.

'Getting on for thirty years now,' Marjac informed her.

She felt a slight sense of relief that it had happened long before she'd met him. 'Does he live here on the island?'

'No, indeed. He went away to the city many a year ago now.'

There was a tense silence between them before Miss Melly struggled to voice the question that was uppermost in her mind. 'I suppose the mother of his son was an island girl?'

Marjac let her knitting lie in her lap, and fixing Miss Melly with a look that was a mixture of sadness and anxiety she replied, 'An island girl, certainly.' Her chin lifted defiantly. 'He is Euan's son and mine.'

'Your son? The one in Glasgow?'

'Indeed.'

Stangely it was less hurtful to know that it was Marjac who had been Euan's lover. She asked herself why she had not suspected a relationship between them.

'It was a long time ago.' Marjac took up her knitting again and seemed glad to unburden herself. 'We were young at the time and would have married but I had to be looking after my parents and working the croft and Euan had his parents and his brother to care for. There was no purpose in our marrying since we could not share a home. When my parents died my uncle – my father's brother–inherited the croft and he and his family moved there. Even had there been room I had no wish to stay with them, and knowing this Alec, my late husband, said would I go and live with him. He'd always shown great affection for me and he was willing to give my child a home, so we married. Alec was a good man to me and he cared for the child as if it had been his own. Our home was as happy a one as any you would have found. But Alec was never strong and though I nursed him with great care and took on all the heavy work of the croft myself it soon became plain he was failing. When he died he left his croft and everything to me so he could be sure I would never be without a home.' She stared for some time at the fire before she spoke again. 'I never loved Alec in the way I'd loved Euan but I believe truly that I made him as happy as any woman could have made him.'

The story Marjac related formed a picture in Miss Melly's mind. The two young lovers; their devotion to their aging parents; their frustration at being separated; the child whom they should have enjoyed together being cared for by another man.

'When your husband, Alec, died could you and Euan not have got married? After all you then had a croft so he could have moved in with you. He could still have looked after his parents, couldn't he?' Miss Melly pointed out.

Marjac was very shocked. 'No island woman would think of taking a second husband,' she retorted with some asperity. 'It is not our way. A woman who marries does so for her lifetime. Even if she was widowed within weeks she would be despised if she took another husband. I have never known such a thing on this island and I'm certain I never shall.' Miss Melly listened in awed silence.

Marjac did not appear at all surprised when she did not make the usual arrangement to return the following summer. She and the other islanders had not been mistaken. Of course it had been Euan who had brought her back year after year and now as she waved her goodbyes from the boat and watched the island recede into the attendant mist Miss Melly doubted if she would ever wish to set eyes on it again.

She still felt bitter that fate had rewarded her ten years of constancy only by allowing her, Theodora Melly, unattractive forty-five-year-old spinster schoolteacher, to discover the thrill of loving without the sureness of being loved in return. The strain of not knowing would continue to haunt her and there would surely be tears in the darkness, so had she gained anything from her experience, she asked herself? Yes! her thoughts leapt to confirm even as she posed the question. There had been times of secret joy and when the ache had dulled perhaps she would be able, without hurt, to return to comforting imaginings of what might have been. There would be no need to repudiate her love, she assured herself gladly. Better a distant loving than none at all . . .

Miss Melly was roused from her meditation by the voices of the cleaners beginning their evening work. She glanced at her watch. She had missed her usual bus and it would be half an hour before there was another one. She opened her desk. Since she would have to clear it before the end of term she might just as well do it now, she thought. At the bottom of the varied piles of books and papers she found a jotter which she had not looked at for some time and, flicking over the pages, she saw the sketches she'd once made of Euan's cottage along with her plans for improving it. Her fingers trembled as she tore out the pages and with fiercely clenched fists screwed them tightly and dropped them into the waste paper basket.

When she reached home she found an exotic picture postcard lying on the mat. It was from Miss Boyd who, having transferred to a school which granted its pupils lengthier vacations, was already on holiday. 'You'd be totally captivated with this place,' Miss Boyd had written. 'Gorgeous *villa à deux*; interesting surroundings and perfect weather. If you're not already holed up on your savage little island, think about joining me. The journey is blissfully uninvolved.'

She propped the postcard beside the clock on the mantelpiece, believing it would offer her no inducement. But before she went to her bed she had resolved that tomorrow she would call at the travel agents on her way home from school.

6

Strange Burden

The stillness of the late afternoon was gently interrupted by the sound of footsteps. Not the clumping of gumboots one was accustomed to hearing but the more refined sound of light-heeled shoes picking a faltering way over the cobbled path that led to my cottage. The sound identified my caller beyond all doubt. In our small crofting community only Miss Beavis wore shoes on weekdays.

'Linny!' I heard her call timidly outside the door that was wide open to the early autumn sunshine. The quaint contraction of my name also proclaimed my visitor to be Miss Beavis. No one else had ever called me Linny.

'Come in,' I responded cheerily. 'I'm just back from milking the cows and the kettle's on for a cup of tea so you've timed your visit nicely.'

Despite being assured of her welcome Miss Beavis entered with a hesitancy that was as much due to shyness as to old age.

'I thought I might have,' she rejoined with a flash of bravado that brought a sudden, impish smile to her wrinkled face. Miss Beavis's frame was spare but her smile I can only describe as bounteous. Without it her features looked prim-set and characterless; when it was released it took complete possession of her face, flicking her eyelids upwards at the same time as her lips widened to reveal large false teeth that had matured to the colour of old ivory. Warming to her smile I grinned back, nodding her towards a chair while I wiped my wet hands on a towel. She steadied herself against the door frame, cleaning her shoes on the folded sack which served for a mat and I noticed, without surprise that she was clutching in her hand a small parcel wrapped in white tissue paper.

'I thought you might be glad to have this,' she said, placing the parcel on the table.

Since she had moved into the neighbouring croft three years previously I had grown used to Miss Beavis bringing me the occasional gift in return for the milk and potatoes with which, in times of plenty, I was able to supply her. Initially I had been much intrigued by the fact that the gifts were invariably wrapped in white tissue paper – an item scarcely used and certainly not easily obtainable within range of our remote Hebridean village. The explanation, I soon discovered, was simple.

Miss Beavis was an expert knitter, working at home for one of the most prestigious city shops. Requiring the garments she sent them to be neatly packed, the shop ensured she was kept liberally supplied with tissue paper.

Though in general Miss Beavis confined her knitting skill to the making of infant clothes – exquisitely fine soft wool layettes, beautifully designed and executed suits and dresses for toddlers – she periodically put aside her more delicate work so as to knit something more robust for me.

'These are perfectly lovely!' I exclaimed, unwrapping the tissue and smoothing a pair of bright red wool mittens over my hands.

'You were saying a wee while ago that mittens would be of more use to you than gloves for some of your croft work,' she reminded me. 'So there they are and I hope you'll find them useful.'

I spread out my fingers for her to see the effect. 'They're so soft and warm,' I enthused. 'Much, much too nice to use for work.'

'Rubbish!' she retorted with mock asperity. 'What would be the sense of giving you coarse-looking mittens that you'd likely wear only to please me? And being that bright colour maybe you'll not find it so easy to lose them,' she added.

I acknowledged the hint of reproof with a small grimace. I am, alas, an inveterate glove loser.

'You really are much too kind,' I told her, pouring out a cup of tea and then adding water since she liked her tea to have only winked at a tea leaf. Because it was Miss Beavis who was taking tea with me I reminded myself to place a saucer under the cup before handing it to her. Like my crofter neighbours I had got into the habit of spurning saucers as non-essentials. She took it with a thin but well-kept hand and, refusing anything to eat, sipped the tea daintily.

Miss Beavis was no crofter. Her background, so far as I knew, was the city, and from sparse references she had made to her past life I had formed the impression that it had been, for the most part, an exceedingly drab and uneventful one, dedicated to the service of two elderly and deeply pious ladies to whom, for forty years until their deaths, she had acted as companion housekeeper.

She seemed to have been always a very solitary person though she had spoken of an elder sister who had married and subsequently emigrated with her husband to Australia. The two had maintained a regular and affectionate correspondence and had been full of plans for a not too distant reunion but, sadly, her sister had died before this could take place. Her sister had left a daughter called Lottie, who was now Miss Beavis's only living relative. It had been Lottie who had wired her aunt with the news of her mother's death and who had, some time later, made the trip to England so as to visit the aunt about whom she had heard so much and yet had not previously met.

'Such a lovely young woman, my niece, and so affectionate to me,' Miss Beavis recalled. 'I was that proud of her.' She was silent for a few moments before continuing. 'She dearly wanted me to go back to Australia with her to live.' There was the faintest tinge of excitement in her voice as if the suggestion alone that she might uproot herself could be considered an adventure.

'But you didn't want to go?' I asked.

'I was tempted,' she replied. 'But I was so afraid I might become a burden. And then I had my two old ladies to look after. I felt I couldn't really leave them to look after themselves after all the years they'd depended on me.' Her smile bloomed suddenly. 'But she made me a promise I'd go to her wedding,' Miss Beavis went on. 'I managed to get a suitable person to look after my ladies and I went to Australia to see her married.'

'And didn't you want to stay once you were there?' I queried.

'I did and yet I didn't,' she said doubtfully. 'In the end I decided it would be better if I stayed with my two old ladies.' There was a wistful finality in her voice which made me suspect the decision had not been such an easy one.

It had been Miss Beavis's two ladies, or more correctly the deaths of her two old ladies, which had been instrumental in bringing her to the cottage in the village.

Hailing originally from the Highlands, the ladies had loyally cherished their connection there and regularly, each summer, they had forsaken their comfortable Manchester home and rented for a few weeks a furnished cottage in the glen where they had spent their childhood. Here Miss Beavis had accompanied them and from the instant she had first set eyes on the mountains and glens, the city-bred Miss Beavis had come under their spell. Recurring visits had increased their enchantment for her until in her mind there had formed a notion, hazy at first but becoming steadily more resistant to her own common-sense arguments, that one day, when she no longer had the old ladies to look after, she herself would buy a cottage in the Highlands where, surrounded by the dramatically beautiful scenery, she could happily spend the rest of her days. When eventually the old ladies had died she found they had left her a small legacy, enough in itself to buy a small cottage so, with her own savings intact, she felt confident enough to place an inquiry in a Highland paper. The result had brought her to the empty cottage on the croft next to my own.

Her arrival had baffled the crofters. Had she been a younger woman they would have quickly categorized her as a member of the current 'back to the land' movement and, anticipating that her efforts would surely provide them with both anecdote and amusement, would have welcomed her if not with warmth then with a kindly interest. But, they questioned, why would an old cailleach like Miss Beavis, not having any thread of connection with anyone in the locality and not being related to anyone within their boundless knowledge of kinship, and at the same time so evidently unfitted to tackle the crofting life, choose to come and live alone in such an isolated place? Surely she would not voluntarily have turned her back on the social life and amenities of the city? They found such behaviour incomprehensible. Steeped as they were in the Highland tradition of help and hospitality for any stranger, yet fearing she might, in time, become too heavy a charge on their good nature, they tended to be cautious in their reception of her, masking their fierce curiosity with a polite but often negligent cordiality.

But right from the beginning Miss Beavis firmly asserted her intention not to become a burden on anyone. An assertion which was repeated often enough for it to have become something of a catchphrase. Wisely reasoning that she was too unsure on her feet to walk far over the rough ground of the crofts, she made no attempt to fraternize with the crofters, my own cottage being as far as she ever ventured. Before long she was being chided for 'making a stranger of herself' but she remained unconcerned, content for the most part with her own fireside and her knitting.

The only involvement with the crofting life she permitted herself was to keep half a dozen hens, and these she cared for most tenderly. Each hen had, in her eyes, a character of its own; each was known to her by name. When the postman mistakenly offered to wring the neck of any hen that was past its useful laying life she was shocked. 'They've served me well,' she reminded him sharply. 'They shall retire in the home they've always known and die when their time comes.'

Such sentiments when relayed to the crofters caused much derisive comment. The village poet felt constrained to compose a poem about an old lady who had a burial ground for hens on her croft with an inscribed tombstone erected in memory of every hen that died. They began to speak of her dismissively as an eccentric, but unless an awesome acceptance of everything life either gave or denied her could be counted as eccentricity I could not agree with their opinion.

'Another cup of tea?' I offered, seeing her cup was empty. 'There's plenty in the pot.'

To my surprise Miss Beavis accepted a second cup, an indulgence she rarely allowed herself even in her own home. I sensed she had something on her mind. While she drank she watched me in an abstracted way as I continued my morning's work – sieving the new milk into a setting bowl and rinsing and scalding the milk pail. After I had carried everything through into the larder and returned to the kitchen she said, 'I really came over to ask would you look after my hens for a few days. That is if you're sure it won't be a burden to you.'

'Of course it won't be a burden,' I assured her. 'I'll do that most willingly. Are you going off on a holiday?' I ended up asking.

'I'm needing to pay a visit to the city,' she explained. 'And I thought I'd best go before the weather turns too cold.'

'That's very wise,' I said. 'Is there anything else I can do for you while you're away?' She shook her head. 'I could light a fire ready for when you get back,' I suggested.

'Oh no, no,' she protested. 'That would be too much of a burden to you.'

'But it really wouldn't be any trouble at all,' I insisted.

'It's very kind of you but no,' she reiterated, too emphatically for me to pursue the suggestion. 'You see I cannot be sure which day I shall be coming back.' She stood up, smoothing down her skirt with fluttering hands. 'You know all about the hens and where I keep the food so I'll get back to my cottage and waste no more of your time.'

I watched her picking her way along the track to her own croft.

It was nearly two weeks later when she called on me again. I thought how much frailer she seemed than when I had last seen her but her smile was bounteous as ever.

'Well, how did you enjoy the city lights?' I greeted her.

'Very well,' she replied. 'But I'd sooner do without them and be back here.' She was rubbing her hands together as if they were cold.

'You really should have let me have a fire going for you ready for when you came home,' I chided her. 'The evenings are getting really chilly. There was quite a frost last night.'

'My fire is not only lit but it was burning merrily when I left it,' she retorted. 'By the time I get back the cottage will be as cosy as if I'd never been away.'

I put down the hod of fuel I was carrying. 'You'll stay and have a cup of tea and a scone while you're here,' I invited. 'And perhaps a boiled egg or two? I made fresh butter yesterday and I've a surfeit of eggs, as you will have guessed. My goodness!' I added. 'Those hens of yours certainly repay their feed. They're splendid layers.'

'I'm glad they weren't a burden to you,' she answered meekly. 'But if you wouldn't mind I'll take just a cup of tea with you. I brought my meal back with me. It needs only to be warmed up and I mustn't stay for fear my fire burns too low and I have to relight it.'

I thought she seemed a little preoccupied, and attributing it to tiredness after her journey refrained from pressing her further. As she put down her cup and saucer and rose to go I saw the faint flush on her sallow cheeks. She was again rubbing her hands together in a slightly agitated way.

'I was wondering,' she surprised me by saying, 'if you're not too busy tomorrow evening would you come and take your tea with me? Latish, I mean, so as not to interfere with your work?'

As she made the request I thought I could guess the reason for her nervousness. We had never been in the habit of issuing mutual invitations to visit. Our relationship was one of easy neighbourliness. We simply dropped in on each other when it seemed necessary or when the mood took us. This, I realized, was going to be something of an occasion.

She went on, 'I've brought a surprise back that I'd like you to share with me, if you will. But,' she added anxiously, 'you mustn't take any notice of my silly ways if it's likely going to be a burden to you.'

'Of course I'll come,' I agreed quickly. 'I shall look forward to it very much.'

It was dusk the following evening when I set out for Miss Beavis's cottage. The day had been dry with a brisk wind and pale sunshine but now the sky was a too flamboyant orange above a ruler-straight line of dark sea. The breeze had died to a reverent whisper as if hushed by the glory of the sunset. Gloomily I suspected it presaged stormy weather.

The two windows of Miss Beavis's cottage were dimly gold behind the drawn curtains and with my hand on the gate I paused, reflecting how the curtained windows and uncluttered surroundings seemed to single out the cottage as if it too was 'making a stranger of itself.'

After rapping lightly on the closed door I lifted the sneck and entered the tiny porch where, silhouetted in the light from the open door of her bedroom, Miss Beavis was waiting, smiling her welcome. I saw she was wearing one of her best dresses and experienced a slight pang of regret that I was not similarly attired in something more festive than the jersey and skirt which had become my normal evening wear once the nights began to grow colder.

'Give me your jacket,' she said, helping me off with it and taking it into the bedroom. She glanced down at my feet and I was glad that I had chosen to wear shoes rather than the shabby but comfortable brogues into which I liked to change after a day in gumboots.

Again I noticed a curious air of excitement in Miss Beavis's manner.

Tentatively she took my arm. 'I want you to do me a little favour and close your eyes for a wee minute till I guide you through into the kitchen. I warned you I had a surprise I wanted you to see so don't open your eyes until I tell you.' Her voice sounded pinched and breathless.

I was intrigued. What on earth has she been up to? I wondered, suspecting the surprise would turn out to be a present for me. Obediently I did as she asked. We took a few short steps together and then a door opened and I knew by the sudden shaft of warmth that we were in the kitchen.

Releasing my arm she placed her hands on my shoulders and turned me to face the way she wanted me. 'Now you can open your eyes!' she announced.

I blinked quickly in the lamplight and as my eyes focused on the table I thought she must have heard my sharp intake of breath as I managed to stifle the unsuitable utterance which rose immediately to my lips. Speechless and bemused, I stared at the bizarre sight which confronted me. Miss Beavis said nothing but I could feel the strain of her impatience to hear some comment from me. But what must I say? What could I say? I knew I must say something.

'What . . .?' I began haltingly and then broke off, the dread of hurting her feelings by saying the wrong thing keeping me temporarily tongue-tied.

'It's a wedding cake,' she said.

It was obviously a wedding cake, but whose? Why? What was it doing here? My mind juggled with possible explanations for its presence.

'Take a closer look at it and tell me do you not think it's beautiful,' she invited shyly.

'It certainly is beautiful,' I agreed, willing the right note of enthusiasm into my voice. I moved closer the better to inspect what was easily the most elaborately decorated wedding cake I had seen for many years. It stood in splendour on an elegant silver base in the centre of the table, its three tiers separated by miniature fluted columns. The snowy white icing of each tier was tastefully decorated with silver leaves, tiny replicas of shoes and bells and all the traditionally lucky charms one associates with weddings. The sides were draped with icing woven as skilfully as fine lace; the top was crowned with a vase of ribbon-tied flowers. Whether deliberately or not Miss Beavis had somehow contrived to place the lamp so that its light fell full on the cake, leaving the rest of the room in shadow. The whole scene had for me a Miss Faversham kind of eeriness.

'It's absolutely superb,' I said with genuine admiration. 'But I must confess, I'm puzzled.' I tried to infuse a note of teasing into my voice. 'Are you going to tell me now that you got yourself married while you were away in the city and any moment now you're going to give me another surprise and produce your new husband?' I glanced over my shoulder towards the door of the bedroom.

'No, no!' she repudiated. 'The cake is mine alone. There is no husband to go with it. We'll have our tea and I will tell the story behind it all.'

The story she told me could no doubt have been duplicated by many young couples who had become betrothed at the outbreak of the first world war. Charles, his name had been, and the day before he was due to leave they had been strolling along the high street looking in the windows of jewellers' shops and trying to decide which engagement ring they wanted when they found themselves looking at the window of a high-class bakery shop where a beautiful wedding cake was on display.

'Oh, I remember it so well,' Miss Beavis told me. 'We were both so taken with it we almost forgot about the ring. I think there must have been at least a dozen other people looking at the same time at the cake but we felt we were the only ones. Charles squeezed my arm and when I turned he was looking at me with such love in his eyes that I can remember it yet as though it was yesterday. "Polly, my love," he said. "I promise you that one day soon you and I are going to have a wedding cake just as grand as that one there. Three tiers and lots of silver decorations. You'd like that, wouldn't you? Don't forget then, Poll. Don't ever forget. This war's not going to last long, everyone says so. I'll be home again soon and then we'll have our own wedding cake. Promise?" So we stood there and promised each other we'd make that day come. It sounds light-hearted of us but we were young and in love and it helped ease the agony of parting when he had to leave me the next morning.'

Her voice trembled a little. 'I think they must have been waiting for him out there because he'd only time to write me just the one letter before he was killed.' Her voice trailed away and then she resumed. 'Enclosed with his letter was a sketch of the wedding cake as he remembered it and on the back he'd written, "Find out how long it will take them to make our cake, Poll, so we can order it as soon as I know I'm coming home."' Her shoulders hunched in a stiff shrug. 'But it wasn't to be. Since then I've never seen a wedding cake without remembering that evening there with Charles and our promise to each other that just such a cake would be ours some day.' Her lips twitched briefly into a regretful pucker.

'So, when the specialist I went to see in the city last week . . .' She paused, hearing my dismayed exclamation. 'Yes,' she admitted. 'It was no holiday I went for but just to have confirmed what the doctor had suspected. It's malignant and it's too late.' She held up her hand as I tried to speak. 'No,' she said. 'Let's not talk about it. It won't be for a while and they'll have me in hospital when it's getting near.'

Our eyes met in understanding.

She continued, 'I was going back to my hotel in the taxi and we were stopped by a traffic jam outside a bakery shop and there in the middle of the window was this gorgeous wedding cake. And such a strange feeling came over me. I couldn't keep the taxi then but all that night I couldn't stop thinking about that wedding cake. I had the feeling that Charles wanted me to make at least that little bit of our dream come true before we were together again. The next morning I took a taxi to the shop but by then the cake had gone from the window. I almost thought the better of it then but I went inside the shop on the pretext of buying some buns and I thought I'd mention the cake that had been in the window and just inquire in a kind of offhand way how much notice they'd want to bake a similar one. When they told me the cake I'd seen was no longer wanted because for some reason the wedding had been cancelled I knew it was meant. I bought it and here it is.'

She looked fondly at the cake. 'And now I'm at last going to cut the wedding cake I should have been cutting, with Charles's hand on mine, fifty years ago.' There was a shiny new knife lying ready beside the cake. I watched her carefully remove the ornaments from the top tier before lifting it on to the table, and found myself holding my breath as she struggled to saw through the icing and cut the first slice – a dauntingly large one which she slid on to my plate. 'I love fruit cake, don't you?' she asked. I didn't, as a matter of fact, but in her excitement she took my faint murmur as assent.

'It's going to take you quite a long time to eat your way through all this cake,' I pointed out, and immediately blushed for my tactlessness.

'Oh, I think I'll last long enough,' she said. 'But you will help me of course. You must take a big chunk of it home with you.'

I tried to demur. Apart from not liking fruit cake as such I had found this one tasted dry, as commercially baked cakes often do and, even had the icing not been too rich for my stomach, I knew I would have little appetite for a cake around which was woven such a poignant story. But she had already cut off a thick slice which she was wrapping in tissue paper.

'I wouldn't want any of the neighbours to get to hear of my foolishness,' she pleaded as she handed me the parcel of cake. 'They'd think me quite daft.'

'They shan't hear it from me,' I pledged.

During the night the slates on the roof began to flutter under the onslaught of the rising wind and by morning the full strength of the gale was upon us, driving before it prolonged showers of heavy rain and pitiless hailstones. Day after day the storm continued, scarcely moderating for more than a quarter of an hour in the twenty-four. The hens had to be confined to their shed for fear they might be blown away. The twice-daily trek to the moors to milk the cows was a wearying battle from which one returned home with one's face scoured by rain, one's body limp and breathless and one's mind obsessed by a yearning to wedge the door firmly against the storm, get into dry clothes and stay indoors.

I saw nothing of Miss Beavis during this time and imagined her snug in her cottage, knitting away happily. Since she allowed herself the luxury of having a daily paper delivered by post each day we had an arrangement that should she need me she would tell the postman who would then deliver the message to me.

It was after a particularly fatiguing sortie with the

weather that I saw the nurse's car in the lane near my cottage and since in our village one never locked one's door I guessed I would find her in the kitchen waiting for me. She quite frequently dropped in while on her rounds for a cup of tea and a chat but when I opened the door and saw her, still wearing a raincoat over her uniform, I knew there was something wrong.

'It's Miss Beavis,' she told me. 'The postman found her awful sick and sent for me. He came over here to tell you but you were still away on the moors.'

'I was. The beasts had hidden themselves away to try and shelter from the storm,' I explained exasperatedly. 'Where is she?' I asked.

'I sent for the ambulance and we got her to hospital,' the nurse said.

'Is it very serious . . . yet?'

The nurse nodded. 'I'm afraid so. I doubt she'll be coming back.'

'I must go and see her,' I said.

'I thought you'd want to do that,' returned the nurse. 'My car's out there waiting so I'll take you as soon as you're ready.'

When I stood beside her hospital bed Miss Beavis seemed to be in no pain. Her eyes were closed but her lids fluttered when I leaned over and spoke to her. For a second or two it seemed as if she were trying to summon up enough strength to give me one of her bounteous smiles.

Her lips moved. 'Lottie . . .' I had to bend closer to hear what she was saying. 'My niece . . . she'll want to know . . . her address . . . on the back of . . . the calendar. But I wouldn't want to be a trouble to anyone.'

I touched her hand to convey to her that I understood and she appeared to slip back instantly into her world of oblivion.

Lottie arrived only in time for her aunt's funeral, there having been difficulties over her flight. She was obviously much distressed that she had been unable to see her aunt while she was still alive so I suggested that instead of returning to the empty cottage she should stay with me.

The following morning she asked if I could spare some time to accompany her to the cottage and to help her sort out her aunt's personal belongings. The cottage and furniture were to be disposed of by the solicitor in charge of Miss Beavis's affairs but there would naturally be some things Lottie herself would want to go through.

We started in the bedroom. I set about the task of folding and packing Miss Beavis's clothes ready for the carrier to take to some charity on the mainland while Lottie selected from among her aunt's more cherished possessions those items which she wished to take back with her to Australia. The bedroom was cold and had the added chill of sadness. Conversation was mostly monosyllabic. It was better when we moved into the kitchen for there we had kept a fire going not only to warm the room but also to burn papers or anything Lottie reckoned was best discarded. It was agreed that I would take any perishables at the same time as I moved Miss Beavis's hens and their food over to join my own flock.

'I do wish I could take some of that china back with me,' said Lottie with a sigh. 'It would be a contant reminder of her. And it is so pretty and old-fashioned.'

'Can't you?' I asked. She shook her head. 'A pity,' I observed. 'She was so fond of it. She would have dearly loved you to have it, I'm sure.'

Again Lottie shook her head. 'Why don't you have it?' she asked.

'I would love to have it,' I replied. 'I'd willingly buy it from you, that is if you're quite sure you can't take it with you.'

'I'm certain I can't take it and I'm just as certain you shall not buy it,' she retorted. 'Next to myself I'm sure there's no one else she would have wanted to have it. I know that from the way she wrote of you in her letters. I would like you to have it,' she added. 'I know you'd cherish it as I would.'

While I was still murmuring my grateful acceptance Lottie went down on her knees beside the dresser and swung open the door of the cupboard. My voice died as I caught sight of the neatly tied carboard box and swiftly there dawned on me a strong suspicion that I knew what it contained.

'I wonder what's in here?' said Lottie, with tiring interest.

Dumbly, as if she were about to discover some guilty secret of my own, I watched her untie the tape of the box and lift the lid. The rustling of tissue paper under her fingers sounded loud in the tenseness of the moment.

'What on earth?' she exclaimed as the wedding cake was revealed. She glanced up at me, her expression one of complete bewilderment. I looked down at her, not knowing what to say. 'This looks like a wedding cake,' she said incredulously. 'It is a wedding cake,' she repeated as she pushed away more of the tissue paper. 'But why would she have a wedding cake here? Was she storing it for someone, do you know?' Her perplexity matched that I had felt when I had first seen the cake.

'It was your aunt's wedding cake,' I told her. 'She brought it back with her after she had been to the city to see the specialist.' Lottie was staring at me. I told her the story Miss Beavis had told me and when I had finished she rose slowly to her feet and the next moment was slumped in a chair beside the table, her head on her arms and her shoulders heaving with deep sobs.

'Poor Mother!' The words were hardly more than a choking gasp. 'Oh, God! Poor lonely Mother,' she repeated brokenly.

I quickly dismissed a faint surprise that her thoughts should be of her own mother. It was natural enough, I supposed. Her mother had been Miss Beavis's sister and the relationship had been a loving one. Lottie was no doubt remembering the reunion the two had planned and which had been destined never to happen.

In the belief that a cup of tea helps to assuage grief I turned to put on the kettle but even as I held it poised above the glowing coals Lottie's voice startled me.

'She was my mother, you know . . . Aunt Polly, I mean, who you knew as Miss Beavis . . . she wasn't my aunt at all . . . she was my real mother . . .'

I put the kettle down more abruptly than I had intended and a little water hissed disapprovingly as it hit the hot embers. I looked askance at Lottie's tear-stained, crumpled face.

'The story she told you about herself and Charles was true enough,' she explained. 'But it didn't end there.' She wiped her eyes and tried to control her voice. 'Charles was my father. That's why I'm named Charlotte, after him. Lottie for short. You see Aunt Polly, that's my mother, was in service at the time and my father was one of the sons of the house where she worked. They fell in love and became secretly engaged.' She held up her right hand. 'This was her engagement ring. She gave it to me when I came over to see her after Mum, that's my Aussie Mum, had died. The truth as to who was my real mother didn't come out until I read a letter Mum had left for me. She told me everything. How Aunt Polly had one day come to her in a very agitated state because she'd found she was pregnant. By that time Charles, my father, had been killed and so she had no one to turn to. She knew she'd get the sack as soon as her condition became obvious and she was far too proud to tell her employers that it was their son who was responsible for her pregnancy. She was sure they would insult her or perhaps accuse her of lying, or both, and for my father's sake she didn't want that to happen.'

Lottie paused to blow her nose and wipe her eyes. Then she resumed. 'Her sister, my Aussie Mum, had been married about three months earlier and she and her husband had made all their plans to emigrate to Australia. Aunt Polly couldn't afford to go with them and since she would never get another job if she had a child to look after they agreed the best thing to do was for her to stay with them until her baby was born – that's me – and then they would pass me off as their own child and take me out to Australia with them. The arrangement was that as soon as Aunt Polly had saved up enough money for her fare or they'd found a job for her to come to she would join them and reclaim me as her own child. That, Aussie Mum said in the letter she left me, was the intention. But when she found she couldn't have children of her own she couldn't bear the idea of giving me up even to my real mother. She'd grown to love me so much, she said, that she truly thought of me as her own child.' Lottie was silent for a time. 'She really did love me, too,' she resumed feelingly. 'There was no doubt about that. Both she and my proxy father thought the world of me and I can understand how they must have been tortured by the thought of having to let me go.

'When eventually Aunt Polly wrote saying she was ready to come out, Mum replied asking her to postpone her visit and pleading to keep me a little longer. She said it would be cruel now to tell me that the Mum and Dad I'd always known were not really my parents. She didn't say in her letter to me how old I was at the time but she admitted to begging desperately for me to be allowed to go on thinking of them as my real parents until I was at least eighteen. I can imagine how heart-rending it must have been for Aunt Polly to receive that letter. All her scraping and saving and yearning and still having to wait to be with her own child! I got an inkling of how much it had cost her to give me up when I came over to see her after Aussie Mum's funeral. I told her then I knew the truth about everything.'

Lottie's elbows rested on the table, cradling her chin. Her eyes stared unseeingly out of the window. 'I can never forget the way she looked at me,' she said quietly. 'I'll admit to having had moments of doubt before I met her. I suppose I blamed her for letting me go. Certainly I felt I had a grievance against her because she'd never written and told me she was my real mother. Nor, and to me it seemed important, had she ever told me how much she loved me.' Lottie screwed her wet handkerchief into a ball and stuffed it in her pocket. From her handbag she took a second handkerchief. 'I suppose that sounds greedy because I'd not suffered any lack of love at any time and I truly loved my Aussie Mum and Dad, so much so that when I first read the letter Mum had left for me I was so shaken I couldn't believe it. I didn't want it to be true. It was awful, really. But gradually my curiosity grew and I made the trip over here. When I met Aunt Polly, as I'd always called her, and saw how like Mum she was and the way her love for me was shining out of her eyes, it seemed to me that my two mothers had fused into one. It wasn't going to be necessary to split my love and loyalty between them. It was a tremendous relief when I realized that.'

I brewed the tea and handed her a cup. After sipping for a few moments she said, 'Did Mother – Miss Beavis – tell you I'd tried hard to get her to come back to Aussie with me to live?' she asked.

'She did indeed,' I replied. 'She was very thrilled that you'd wanted her with you.'

'But she wouldn't leave her old ladies,' Lottie said.

'She was a very loyal person, I think,' I told her. 'And she did get to see you married.'

'Yes,' Lottie admitted. 'And I can see her now, standing beside Dad who was not my real Dad and shaking hands with the guests as she was being introduced not as the mother of the bride but as "Lottie's closest living relative". God! How ironic!' Lottie covered her face with the palms of her hands. 'I would have been proud to announce her as my mother. You said she was loyal, didn't you? Well it was out of loyalty to her sister that she insisted on being known as the aunt of the bride.'

Lottie had finished her first cup of tea and I handed her a second.

'I wish more than ever she'd stayed in Aussie with us when she came for the wedding,' she said. 'I'm sure she would have been happy there.'

I said, 'If it's any comfort to you she said to me more than once that she wished you could have seen her here in her cottage. She said you would have been more content to know how happy she was with the way things had turned out.'

'I'm glad she was happy,' said Lottie. 'As a matter of fact I was planning to come over next year and bring the children to see her.'

'Yes,' I acknowledged. 'She was certainly looking forward to that.'

'And now she's dead without ever having set eyes on her

own grandchildren or they on her.' She got up and emptied the remains of her tea into the sink. 'If only she'd stayed with us,' she repeated.

'She was so determined not to become a burden to anyone,' I pointed out. 'It was her one great fear.'

'How little I knew of her,' Lottie said, kneeling and gently pushing back the tissue over the cake. 'What a long time to have cherished a dream,' she murmured. 'But what happens to that dream now?' She looked questioningly at me. 'I can't possibly take this back to Australia with me, can I?'

'I shouldn't expect it to carry well,' I agreed.

'Could I give it to someone locally?'

'Oh no,' I said emphatically. 'She begged me not to let the village get to hear of it.'

'No, of course not,' Lottie was quick to agree. We looked at each other reflectively. What could one do with two tiers of an unwanted wedding cake?

'Do you think if we cut it into wedges and distributed it among the crofters without telling them what it was they'd accept it without any questions?'

'I'm positive they won't,' I told her. 'They'd be far too curious.' I was envisaging myself landed with the task of delivering a piece of wedding cake to every croft in the village and having to think up some plausible explanation as to why I was doing it. They would have been certain to disregard my explanation and come up with a far more colourful one of their own. It was more than likely I would be suspected of being a jilted bride. I did not fancy the situation one little bit.

Lottie frowned. 'Let's brew up another pot of tea,' she suggested. 'It might help us to think of something.' But neither of us could come up with a satisfactory solution to the problem.

'There's simply no more time to think about it,' she said, putting the lid back on the box. With some misgivings I realized I was going to have to offer to take over responsibility for disposing of the cake.

Lottie left early the following morning on the first stage

of her long journey, leaving me the key of Miss Beavis's cottage. As soon as I was back from the morning milking I went over to the cottage and carried back the box containing the wedding cake and at the same time I packed and brought over the china which Lottie had insisted I have. The china I set out on the shelves of my own dresser but the cake I took through to the larder and put it in a cupboard where it would be safe from curious eyes until I could come up with a suitable way of disposing of it. A couple of weeks went by and each time I needed to open the cupboard the sight of the box reproached me for my continuing indecision. But what could one do with an unwanted wedding cake, the existence of which had to be kept secret?

The cake was both too heavy and too fragile to be posted and I rejected the idea of consigning it by road to some charity because not only were our roads like obstacle courses but our carrier tended to be exuberant in his treatment of packages. In addition his lorry was an ancient jouncer and as the cake would then have to be transferred to a ferry and then to the luggage van of a train I saw little prospect of it arriving at its ultimate destination in any state but crumbs.

I found the address of a children's home, located at a safe distance from the village, and offered the cake to them, at the same time asking if they would be responsible for its collection. They thanked me for my offer but politely declined it, pointing out that not only would transportation be both costly and difficult but, in their opinion, rich wedding cake could not be considered suitable fare for young children.

I wrote to an old people's home. The matron replied on a sour note, not thanking me for my offer but simply informing me that since the home was run exclusively for elderly ladies she could not imagine a wedding cake being of any conceivable use to them. She added that if I wished to be generous they would accept a cash donation in lieu.

My dilemma remained and whichever way my mind turned over the problem there came no flash of inspiration. Of course I could have dumped it in the sea when no one was looking; or I could have dug a hole and buried it on the croft, but I abhor waste and by this time the cake had acquired such an identity of its own I shrank from getting rid of it in such a barbarous way. So, Micawber like, I let the days go by, waiting for something to turn up.

A letter arrived from Lottie telling me she had arrived home safely and thanking me for my friendship with her mother. She added a postscript: 'I do hope the cake did not prove to be a burden to you.' Her words brought me up with a jolt. It was as though Miss Beavis had been speaking. The cake had indeed become a burden and, I admitted to myself, was becoming increasingly so as each day passed. And how Miss Beavis would have loathed that.

It was the receipt of my first Christmas card that triggered off my idea.

The crofters did not recognize Christmas as a festival but they celebrated New Year with such wild enthusiasm that by midnight on New Year's eve there was never a sober man in the village. Except for the traditional black bun no food was allowed to interfere with the serious business of whisky drinking. My idea was a quite simple one.

Black bun – or Scots bun as it is sometimes called – is a moist fruit cake mixture enclosed in a pastry case and baked in the oven. If I chipped off most of the icing and then mashed and soaked the cake in plenty of brandy for a few days before wrapping it in pastry and baking it lightly I was confident I could pass off the result to the inebriated first footers as my version of black bun. Congratulating myself that my difficulty was at last resolved and that, could she have known, Miss Beavis herself would have smiled her bounteous smile and considered it fitting that her cake should be consumed during an evening of revelry, I went cheerfully into the larder and opened the cupboard.

But it was too late!

As I drew the box containing the cake towards me, I saw to my horror the tell-tale signs of mice in the space behind it. The corner of the box was now a nibbled mousehole. Gingerly I lifted the lid. As I feared, much of the tissue wrapping was shredded like confetti and I recoiled with disgust when I uncovered the cake and saw the icing liberally bestrewn with mice droppings. For some moments I stood, shocked and dismayed by the sight. And then, slowly, quite slowly, elation returned. I no longer had a problem!

Taking the cake through to the kitchen I dropped it whole into the hens' mash bucket. After I had poured plenty of hot water over it and pounded it vigorously with an empty cider flagon, it had become a steaming and unidentifiable pulp.

When I took it out to the hens, including those which had been Miss Beavis's pets and which had by this time incorporated amicably with my own flock, they were already clustered round the gate of their pen. The afternoon was cold and growing rapidly colder. There were great shawls of cloud drifting in from the sea and already a few snowflakes were threading themselves among the breeze which was beginning to whine with icy intent around the corners of the sheds.

'There! That should keep you warm and well fed,' I told the hens as I tipped up the pail of still steaming mash. I lingered for a little while watching as they attacked it with hasty greed and wondering what effect if might have on their egg-laying. I looked towards Miss Beavis's croft which was as yet unsold. The cottage was dark and empty. With a shrug I left the hens to their guzzling and returned to the cosy warmth of the kitchen to begin my own Christmas preparations.

And to set a mouse trap in the larder cupboard.

7

The Last Shot

Only the sound of gull cries, thinned by distance, and the muffled crowing of the cockerel from inside the poultry shed broke the early morning silence of the croft. Outside the cottage the boy stood, narrowing his eyes against the daring shaft of sunshine that was doing its utmost to pierce the bulwark of mist which lay unyielding over the hills.

Meg, his collie dog, shook herself, stretched and then fixed her eyes on her master, eager to divine his intentions even before he should utter a word of command. Disregarding her the boy went over to the byre and, collecting a spade, leaned it against the stone dyke while he re-entered the cottage. Meg, knowing the day's work or play – she cared not which – would shortly begin, again waited outside, her ears pricked, her tail waving confidently as she listened to every sound. When the boy emerged carrying a gun under his arm, she began to prance around him. Meg was always ready for a hunt.

Picking up the spade and with Meg at his heels the boy strode purposefully in the direction of the tall clump of rowan trees which indicated the moor entrance to the croft and, reaching it, he threw the spade over the earth dyke and then clambered over cautiously, holding the gun. Meg leapt cleanly after him and together boy and dog followed the sheep track which wound across and down the hillside towards the noisy, swollen burn. When after a few hundred yards the boy left the track and made for a well-concealed corrie among the hills Meg, as if she knew where they were now bound for, raced ahead, looking back every few moments as if she expected to hear a word of restraint. When she heard none she ran further ahead, looking back less frequently to assure herself that he was still following her. The boy plodded on looking neither to right nor left but still carrying the spade over his shoulder and the gun under his arm.

When they came to a secluded area of swampy grass surrounded by rampant heather the boy stopped, placed his gun on a dry tussock and with the spade cut the sods from a patch roughly three feet square. These he carefully laid aside before commencing to dig out the exposed earth. Quiveringly Meg watched him, anticipating the command to 'seek' the quarry that would soon bolt, but when there was no result she sat down a few feet away content to watch and await his next instruction.

When the hole was about three feet deep the boy picked up the gun, loaded it and called her. Meg ran to the edge of the hole and peered down but, unable to either see or hear anything worth hunting, she looked up at him, puzzled that he was giving her no further directions. The boy bade her sit and instantly she obeyed him, watching and waiting for his slightest whisper of command. He raised the gun and fleetingly his agonized eyes met the steadfast gaze of his dog in a last brief farewell. Focusing on the centre of the heart-shaped white patch between her eyes, he pulled the trigger. He thought he had glimpsed a second of bewilderment before her life had ended and she had fallen, a writhing black carcase, into the newly dug grave. Laying down the gun he lurched half blindly towards a tumble of boulders, but his knees gave way before he reached them and he collapsed on to the damp turf where the grief he had been compelled to deny himself erupted into a convulsive sob compounded by a retching and vomiting that continued until he thought he could have no stomach left.

Turning on his side, he looked out to sea where the mist was rolling inexorably towards the land. Soon the glen would be swamped by its grey caress. His eyes burned and his head ached, and pulling handfuls of the cool damp grass he held them to his forehead and to his closed lids. When he woke he realized he was wet through. He was not conscious of being cold but only of being enclosed in the stillness and soundlessness that presses itself over a mist-shrouded land.

He sat up, hugging his knees and blinking repeatedly in an effort to clear his vision before he got to his feet.

Then he walked reluctantly to the open grave and forced himself to look down into it. Already the rain which had soaked through his homespuns while he slept had plastered the rough black hair of Meg's coat against her body as he had never seen it do in life. He should have covered her! The thought smote him and yet he knew he'd been incapable of doing any such thing at the time. His eyes were drawn to her now half closed ones and he imagined she was still looking at him, reproaching him for his treachery. Her mouth too was partly open, the pink tongue visible as if it might at any time respond to her panting. In his mind's eye he saw her again sitting, as he had bade her, and looking at him trustingly as she'd faced her death, and with the memory came the perplexity that such an intelligent dog should have appeared to have no premonition of the fate that was to befall her. Blunderingly he reached for the spade and commenced to fill in the grave.

It was 'the Woman' who was to blame, he raged to himself as he worked. The Woman he'd decided to hate ever since the day she had stepped into his life after his mother had died. The Woman whom he could now hate with even more intensity.

He'd been eight years old when his mother died, and the anguish of it still racked him. She had gone so suddenly that there had been no chance to say goodbye to her. No chance to tell her how much he loved her. Not even a chance to see her in death.

He'd been spending the summer holiday from school with his Aunt Netta and Uncle Hamish who lived up at the north end of the island where Uncle Hamish was head gamekeeper on a large estate. He'd thoroughly enjoyed that holiday, accompanying his uncle on his daily tours of inspection, observing his skill at tracking and his knowledge of wild things and, best of all, his expert shooting.

Within a very short time he'd developed such a keenness to learn how to handle a gun that his uncle went to the length of borrowing an air rifle from the son of one of the under-keepers and let him practise shooting, first at a target and then, as his aim improved, at the occasional rabbit. The boy resolved then that when he was older he too would become a gamekeeper.

Shortly before he was due to return home he and his uncle were out on the hill looking for foxholes when, in the distance, they heard a rifle shot. Since shooting on the estate was strictly forbidden save with the owner's or the game-keeper's permission, his uncle immediately fired an answering shot into the air. There was no sound of further shots but his uncle, muttering about poachers, began to stride in the direction from which he reckoned the shot had come. After a little time he put his hands to his mouth and shouted loudly and as they listened there came an answering shout.

'It was just a way of calling my attention,' his uncle explained. 'Maybe the laird's turned up all of a sudden or maybe it's the income tax mannie,' he added wryly. Within a few minutes they saw one of the under-keepers, beckoning as he came towards them. 'Ach, he has a message for me seemingly,' his uncle said, and telling the boy to stay where he was, he went forward to meet the man.

The boy watched them confer for a few seconds but, since from their attitudes it seemed to him there was no urgency about the message, he turned his attention to following a small herd of deer who were grazing their way up the mountain. When he looked back the under-keeper had already left and his uncle was coming towards him.

'Nothing serious?' the boy called, thinking perhaps that the under-keeper had been asking for a day off to visit his wife who was expecting their twelfth baby. But as his uncle drew closer he saw by his expression that the message had been serious indeed. 'What is it?' the boy asked. 'Not Aunt Netta?' For a strained moment or two his uncle did not answer him. Then he said, 'We'd best sit down for a wee whiley, laddie.'

And it was there, sitting out on the hillside with a gentle breeze blowing through his hair and his uncle beside him, that the boy was given the news of his beloved mother's death. He was so stunned that for several minutes he was unable to take in the meaning of his uncle's gruff, halting words. Had he really said his mother was dead? But she couldn't be, he assured himself. There'd been not a thing wrong with her when she'd seen him off on the bus at the beginning of his holiday and there'd been no word from his father that she'd been taken ill. If that had been so his father would surely have sent a message to Mrs McInnes at the post office and Mrs McInnes would somehow have managed to get word to Aunt Netta for him to come home immediately. With disbelief pounding at his mind he turned to his uncle with wide pleading eyes. 'It's not really true, is it? She can't be dead! Not my mother?'

His uncle shook his head gravely. 'I fear it is true right enough, laddie, and it would be my dearest wish to tell you that it was not so.' He gave way to a heavy sigh. 'Such a beautiful woman your mother. Beautiful in every way,' he added.

The boy shivered, as if he'd suddenly felt that he'd been encased in a jacket of ice. His uncle darted a concerned look at him. 'Now you're not going to cry, are you laddie? Not a big brave young fellow like yourself?'

With a stifled 'No!' the boy jumped to his feet and began to run, not caring where he was making for so long as it would be away from the stark reality of his uncle's words. Not until he caught his foot in a concealed rabbit hole and fell face down did he cease his wild flight and there he lay gasping and sobbing, letting the short cropped grass absorb his tears.

It was his uncle's tribute to his mother's beauty which had filled him with the need to escape. He'd always thought his mother beautiful. No one could have considered her as being less than beautiful, he told himself as through his mind there had floated the gentle image of her. He pictured her smiling at him and at his father, her gentle eyes aglow with the love she had for them. He pictured then the way his father's normally stern features would so easily relax into tenderness when he looked at her.

The sudden vision of his father racked him with further anguish. He must get back home as soon as he possibly could, he resolved, and sped swiftly towards the track which would lead him back to his uncle's house. As he ran he planned his next move. He would catch the daily bus tomorrow and then by afternoon he'd be joining his father.

To his dismay his Aunt Netta reminded him that the next day was the Sabbath and since the bus did not run on the Sabbath and there was no alternative method of transport it would not be before the Monday afternoon that he would reach his home.

When the bus deposited him at the end of the lane that led to their croft his father, his face haggard with grief, was waiting to meet him. Automatically the thought had flashed across his mind that it only needed his mother to smooth away the lines of suffering, but in the same instant the truth hit him like a cudgel and he had to turn a sob into a cough to deceive his father.

Except for a quiet 'Well laddie!' he and his father exchanged no greeting until they reached the entrance to the croft. Then his father halted and put a gentle hand on his son's shoulders. 'Your mother was buried this day,' he said in a voice that began steadily but broke into a sharp whisper. 'I'm right sorry you didn't get the chance to see her first but the weather was that hot it wasn't possible to keep her.' The boy needed no further explanation. Having grown up with the knowledge that since it was both impractical and unhealthy in hot weather to try to keep a corpse in the limited space available in a small snug croft house, death had inevitably to be followed by swift burial.

He felt confused by his own reaction to the knowledge that his mother had already been buried; whether he was angry that the intervening Sabbath had prevented him from seeing her or whether he was relieved that it had saved him from seeing her lying still and lifeless and no longer able to look at him with love in her dark eyes.

He dreaded entering the kitchen which, without her, struck him as being like an empty picture frame, and though its familiar furnishings proclaimed it as being his home he felt it had ceased to be the place where he could truly belong. Without his mother everything in the room seemed to have withdrawn itself. The kettle and pots and pans seemed to protest that it was her right to use them. The cups and plates which filled the dresser were still so much hers that when his father brewed tea and suggested he could set the table he felt diffident about taking them from the dresser.

It was not until after they had drunk their tea and eaten a few shop biscuits from the tin that his father made a visible effort to comfort him. Still sitting with his folded arms on the table and looking down at his toil-worn hands, he said in a voice roughened with emotion, 'You'll need to try thinking of me as your mother as well as your father, laddie. It'll be the best we can do for each other now.'

Unable to speak, the boy nodded sadly. He longed desperately for his father to look at him at that moment, to meet his eyes and to see in them the same tender caring he'd seen in the glances he'd exchanged with his mother. But his father did not look at him and the boy turned away, fearful of embarrassing him by allowing his wretchedness to overwhelm him or, worse still, risk breaching what he was certain was his father's iron control over his own deep despair. The boy never doubted the strong bond between himself and his father but since earliest childhood he had absorbed the knowledge that his father was a Highlander and that even between close relatives, affection was not displayed and that understanding must be masked by impassivity. Impressed by the tolerance and wisdom that lay beneath his attitude and grim reserve, the boy had striven to be like him. Now, he resolved, the time had come for him to strive even harder; and in the months following his mother's death, he began to believe that he was successfully armouring himself with an outward stoicism that might one day equal his father's.

Just before the spring school holidays were due to commence his father received a letter from Aunt Netta and Uncle Hamish suggesting that the boy might like to pay them another vist. 'Ach, seeing they've never had bairns of their own I daresay they'd dearly like to have some young company for a while,' his father encouraged.

'Very well,' the boy agreed in a tone that had sounded dutiful though in truth he'd been hoping for just such an invitation.

He stayed almost a month with his uncle and aunt and, save for a lurking worry that because he had learned of his mother's death while he'd been on holiday fate might deal him a similar blow and give him news of some mishap to his father, his spirits lightened with each day that had passed. Shortly before he was due to return home his uncle said to him one evening, 'Go and take a look in the shed at the back, laddie. There's something there you might be wishing to take back with you.'

Concealing his eagerness the boy went out to the shed and found there, lying on an old table, a gun such as the one his uncle allowed him to use when they were out shooting together. It couldn't be for him, he decided, and looked around the shed to see what other thing of interest there might be. He saw nothing. Hesitantly he picked up the gun and took it back into the house.

'Well, laddie!' his uncle said, glancing up from the book he'd been reading.

'D'you mean I can take this home with me?' the boy asked.

His uncle nodded, his eyes seeming to reflect the shine in the eyes of the boy. 'Aye, so,' he confirmed. 'It's not new, as you can see for yourself, but it's been kept well oiled and cleaned so I reckon you'll get some good sport from it yet.'

Jubilant at the thought of possessing a gun of his own the boy took it outside and practised balancing it on his arm and squinting along the barrel. 'It's not loaded and maybe your father won't allow you to shoot at anything but a target until you're a bitty older, but I'm thinking you'll soon be making a crack shot,' his uncle told him.

As he expected, his father was waiting to meet him when he stepped off the bus. Proudly he handed him the gun and waited for his comments. 'Are you telling me this belongs to you?' His father's eyebrows rose in what the boy had strongly suspected was feigned surprise. He was fairly certain his uncle would not have given him the gun without first asking permission from his father. 'Well.' He looked through the barrel. 'I must say your Uncle Hamish is mighty good to you,' he commented.

'Aunt Netta's awful good to me too,' the boy said. 'There's a great pile of girdle scones and bannocks in my bag as well as a leg of mutton she's cooked for us. Aunt Netta's a pretty good cook,' he commended her.

'She is?' his father said so tautly that the boy immediately chided himself on his thoughtlessness. His own mother had been a wonderful cook. They walked the rest of the way in silence.

The track through the croft was squelchy after a heavy shower and as they stamped the mud from their boots before entering the cottage the boy heard the high-pitched yapping of a puppy. He looked enquiringly at his father. 'Who's in there?' he whispered, thinking his father might have asked a neighbour to prepare a meal in readiness for him.

'There's a young collie bitch inside waiting for you to go in and tell her you're to be her master,' his father said with studied nonchalance.

With an exclamation of joy the boy rushed into the kitchen and, laying his cherished gun on the bench knelt down and took the puppy in his arms. 'My but she's a good one,' he permitted himself to enthuse. 'Is she truly to be mine?'

'She's yours,' his father confirmed. 'And she's a good one right enough. Her mother's won more than a prize or two at the trials.' Looking down at him his father continued, 'Just see now that you take good care of her and train her the right way.'

'I'll do that surely,' the boy promised, holding the fat and exuberant puppy a little away from him so as to inspect her markings. She was all black save for a roughly heart-shaped patch between her eyes and a white tip to her tail. 'See that!' he bade his father as the puppy climbed to nestle her head against his neck. 'She's clever! See how she knows already she belongs to me!' His voice was sharp with excitement and when he looked up suddenly to gauge his father's admiration their eyes met and for a few seconds held their gaze. And at last the boy saw there the same tender regard as there had been for his mother.

'You'll have to give her a name,' his father pointed out.

'She's going to be Meg,' the boy replied decisively.

So the boy acquired his dog and his gun within a few days of each other and with their aid his mourning for his mother gradually become less poignant.

Meg's herding instinct quickly manifested itself even as a puppy and it was not long before she made a game of rounding up virtually anything that moved. Chickens which strayed from their pen were relentlessly driven back and several times daily the more adventurous ducks were shepherded into a line and made to waddle protestingly back to their shed and, though she was considered too young to be trained to gather sheep, her keenness to do so was never in doubt. Apart from instant obedience to his orders she hardly needed training, the boy assured himself.

When, the following spring, he again visited his Uncle Hamish and Aunt Netta he was allowed to take Meg with him and there he proudly demonstrated not only Meg's obedience but also her intuitive understanding of his intentions. His uncle was very impressed.

'Aye, you have the makings of a fine dog there,' he acknowledged. 'She's maybe just a wee bitty over-eager but no doubt she'll calm down as she gets older.'

'Ach, I'm not wanting to train her as a working dog,' the boy demurred. 'It's more for a companion I want her. And to go shooting with me when I'm wanting a rabbit or two.'

'It would be a waste not to train her,' his uncle advised. 'Any dog with an instinct for sheep should rightly be trained for fear it might go wild.'

The boy was speaking the truth when he told his uncle he had no plans to train Meg seriously, but so keen was she to prove her desire to work that his ideas changed and, when she reached the recommended age for training to begin, he approached the shepherd and asked him if he would allow them to sometimes accompany him when he was herding so Meg could learn from his older and more experienced dogs. The shepherd himself was impressed by her early signs of mastery over the flock and confirmed that, save for a small fault of over-eagerness which he admitted could soon be corrected, Meg showed promise of being at least as good as any other sheepdog in the area.

The boy conveyed the shepherd's opinion to Uncle Hamish next time he visited and, touched by his earnestness, his uncle persuaded the estate shepherd to allow him to work some of the laird's sheep. The shepherd judged her performance near faultless.

'Aye,' his uncle approved. 'She'll be a credit to you yet, will that dog.'

It was on that same visit that he was provided with ammunition and permission to hunt rabbits over a circumscribed area of the estate without his uncle's supervision, and subsequently he spent a good deal of his time wandering the hills and probing the secrets of unfamiliar corries and, between bouts of hunting, absorbing the knowledge of the ways of wild creatures, knowledge which his uncle warned him he would need if he was ever to fulfil his ambition to become a gamekeeper. Meg proved to be the loyal and intelligent companion he hoped she'd be, contentedly walking at his heels when he bade her to do so; happily flushing out rabbits when he gave her the instruction to 'chase!' and when, after a picnic lunch in some sheltered spot he rested drowsily for a while, she settled herself to guard him, ears and eyes alert and stiffening like a pointer whenever she scented or perceived something she thought he ought to be made aware of.

On one such expedition he was taking his usual rest beside a reed-bordered lochan and lazily scanning the horizon to judge the weather prospects for the evening when he noticed a sluggish dark cloud heaving itself over the rugged shapes of the outer islands. The islands are having a good squall to themselves, he thought and wondered if the squalls would bring others in their wake and in which direction they would move. Overhead the sun was still shining but out towards the horizon the sea was darkened by wind ripples. As he watched he involuntarily recalled how he and his Uncle Hamish had been resting not so far away from this very spot when they heard the shot that heralded the appearance of the under-keeper bringing the calamitous news of his mother's death. Suddenly the cloud seemed to have taken on an air of menace and for a long, tense moment he was haunted by a superstitious worry that something had gone wrong. But then Meg, sensing his fear, began to lick his face with such determin-ation that he chuckled as he pushed her away. When he looked again at the cloud it had already drifted away northwards without so much as a temporary interruption of the sunshine.

Returning to his uncle's home later that evening and gloating inwardly on his excellent bag of rabbits, he heard his uncle's voice hailing him from one of the sheds. Believing it to be a shout of congratulation, he held up the rabbits for inspection.

'My but you've done well, laddie,' his uncle approved. Beckoning him into the shed he urged, 'Hang them on the beam there and then go away into the house and have a word with your Aunt Netta. She's a little something she wants to say to you,' he added, and winked mysteriously.

For a moment the boy stood stock still staring compell-ingly at his uncle, willing him to explain why his aunt should want him. His throat dried and the worry he'd experienced when he saw the cloud returned to clamp his stomach.

'Has there been an accident?' he jerked out sharply. 'My father?'

'No no, laddie. Your father's just fine. There's nothing wrong. Nothing at all.' His emphasis did not reassure the boy and he continued to stare at his uncle doubtfully. 'Just you go into the house now and hear what your aunt has to say to you,' his uncle insisted.

Puzzled, the boy walked stiffly over to the house and entered the kitchen where his Aunt Netta was sitting at the table casually flicking through the household linens pages of a thick mail-order catalogue. When she saw him she pushed it aside, and taking off her spectacles she regarded him solemnly. 'Well, laddie,' she began, 'I've had word from your father today and he says I'm to tell you that you now have a new mother.' Seeing the boy's eyes widen she paused for a moment. She'd dreaded having to tell him and her voice, which she'd managed to keep composed at first, had become unsteady. 'He says I'm to tell you she is a very nice woman and also very kind and she is looking forward to being your new mother and welcoming you back home.'

Too numbed even to gasp, the boy stood rigid. A new mother! He felt outraged that his father could have said such a thing and that his aunt should have repeated it. How could he ever have a new mother? His mother was dead and had been buried for two years. He could never forget her and he'd believed his father could never forget her, yet now he had married another woman and was attempting to substitute her for his mother. It was unthinkable! Of course he'd overheard some of the neighbours periodically urge his father to take another woman into the home but he'd been certain his father had scorned their suggestions. 'A boy of that age still needs a mother,' he'd heard them say and had felt so angry and insulted on both his own and his father's behalf that he'd had to restrain himself from rushing at them and shouting that neither he nor his father would be crazy enough to want anyone else in his mother's place. He'd believed he and his father were now partners; that no one should ever be allowed to come between them; and indeed his mind had so steadfastly rejected the possibility of there ever again being a woman to share their home that no fragment of doubt had remained there.

He remained still, gaping speechlessly at his aunt and she, made uneasy by his unswerving gaze, rose from her chair and reaching up took his father's letter from the mantelpiece. Glancing over it as if seeking confirmation she said, 'Your father doesn't make a mention of who this woman might be nor even if she's an island woman, but being the man he is and has always been he will not have chosen unwisely.'

126

The boy kept up his stony silence.

'Laddie,' she tried to reason with him. 'Laddie you must try to understand how hard it's been for your father with no woman beside him and it must have been harder still for him to have been left alone with a motherless son to raise.'

The dismay in the boy's eyes silenced her but at last he found his voice. 'I will have no new mother and if it could be managed I would wish to stay here with you and Uncle Hamish rather than go back to my father and his new woman,' he stated firmly and, calling to Meg, he went to seek solace by fiercely pitching stones into the nearby river.

As he'd expected, when he got off the bus his father was waiting to meet him and he was relieved to see there was no woman beside him. Ever since he'd said goodbye to his aunt and uncle he'd been dreading there might be. Dreading that because there would be witnesses he would have had to pretend to a cordiality he could not feel.

His father greeted him with his usual abruptness but when they reached the entrance to the croft he paused. 'We'll stay here and say what we have to say to each other before we go into the house,' he said. So they sat down on the dyke and there was a tense silence between them for some time before his father spoke. 'Your aunt will have told you about the woman I have married and who would like you to think of her as your mother?' The boy nodded dispiritedly. 'She's a good woman and was a teacher for a while to two boys in Oisgill so she will be well able to understand you.'

'Where did you get this woman?' the boy asked bluntly.

'She's from Luig,' his father answered and as if he thought it might temper his son's obvious antipathy he added, 'She and your mother used to know each other when they were children.' One of the boy's hands was resting on Meg's neck, the other began pulling savagely at heather stalks. His father slid a brief look at him. 'What we have to settle now is what you will be calling her,' he enjoined.

'I will never call her Mother!' the boy was quick to declare. 'Never, never will I call her Mother!' he reiterated.

His father considered for a moment before acknowledging, 'No, maybe that would be asking too much of you, but since she is to share our home and look after us and since she is my wife now there is need for you to call her something.'

The boy shrugged. 'To me she will be the Woman. I will call her just that.'

'You will not!' His father's voice was sterner than he had ever heard it. 'However much you disapprove, I now have another wife and I insist you respect her. I will permit no discord in the home. Her name is Molly and since you do not wish to call her Mother I think she will not be displeased if you call her that.'

The boy turned to face him. 'Why did you marry her?' he demanded rebelliously. 'Have you not been content with our life together? Have you forgotten my mother so easily?'

'Stop!' His father's command was so sharp that the boy flinched away from him and, covering his face with his hands, he shut out the light and imagined his mother smiling at him. When he dropped his hands he saw from his father's expression how deeply the words had cut him.

'Perhaps you will understand some day.' His father excused himself with such an air of desolation that the boy wanted to apologize and comfort him.

'I will call her Molly,' he yielded sulkily, though he vowed to himself that he would never think of her as anything but the Woman.

'Very well,' his father accepted.

She was waiting at the door of the cottage to meet them – a plumpish, smiling figure wearing a brightly patterned overall. Reluctantly the boy submitted to her warm handshake. 'Well now,' she greeted him, 'I'm pleased to be welcoming you to your home,' He'd feared she would offend him by being effusive but on the contrary her manner, though warm, betrayed a trace of anxiety. She stood aside as he and his father entered the kitchen where the table was laid ready for a meal. 'Your father told me you had a great liking for salt herring and potatoes so that's what I have for you. I hope you'll find my cooking to your liking.'

The boy murmured a faint acknowledgement while

thinking grumpily that he wouldn't like them as much as his mother's. While he ate he watched her covertly as she moved about the kitchen. How could his father ever have imagined that this woman could begin to compare with his mother? His mother had been dark and slim and lithe. This woman was fair and fat and awkward. He hated the idea of her sharing his home. Hated the prospect of having to talk to her. But for his father's sake he had to pretend an acceptance of her. So, when he had to be polite he addressed her as Molly but mostly he got away with not calling her anything at all.

Time had not lessened his resentment and yet, grudgingly, he had to allow that, other than being his father's second wife, she'd done her best to give him no cause to resent her. Indeed she was unfailingly kind and considerate towards him, placidly ignoring his persistent rejection of her friendly overtures; never upbraiding him for his frequent and sometimes deliberate carelessness; never at any time attempting to impose herself between him and his father and never criticizing their established pattern of living. It irritated him to notice that the neighbours and even his friends had quickly warmed to her easygoing manner and her desire to be of help. It irritated him even more to discern that Meg had developed a trusting affection for her but, despite his observations and despite the fact that the Woman, as he still thought of her, proved to be a hard and cheerful worker both in the house and on the land, his own attitude towards her remained one of implacable hatred. He was relieved that at least his father had not chosen a useless woman, and though he sometimes saw him give her a nod of approval after she had completed a task to his satisfaction, it pleased the boy that he never saw his father look at 'her' in the same way that he'd been used to looking at his mother.

At the end of the long summer holiday the scholars returned to school to find they had a new schoolmistress, the old one having retired at the end of the previous term. The new mistress had brought with her a nondescript terrier dog which, in addition to shrill ear-piercing yapping, displayed a tendency to sink its sharp teeth into the ankles of anyone who came near it. Since the general footwear was sturdy gumboots the children endured its attacks and simply retaliated with a kick but the crofters, concerned for their sheep and cattle, worried about its presence in their midst, particularly when it became evident that the schoolmistress appeared to have little or no control over it. Before she had been there three weeks the shepherd warned her that if ever he found her dog loose on the hill he would shoot it on sight.

The schoolmistress went with her woes to the Woman and subsequently there sprang up a friendship between the two. Often, as the days shortened, the boy went home to find the schoolmistress having a strupak in the kitchen while her dog, though restrained by collar and lead, snarlingly provoked the innocent Meg from under its owner's chair.

One day during that term the boy arrived home from school to find a letter from his Uncle Hamish asking if he thought his father could spare him just for two or three days to give Aunt Netta and him a hand. Just as the laird had arrived for the deerstalking hadn't one of his best ghillies gone sick and then another one had been called to the hospital where his wife had given birth to a baby. To cap it all the cook at the Big House had fallen and broken her leg so Aunt Netta had needed to take over in the kitchen, so now there was no one to give him a hand with his own animals and one cow nearing calving. 'But,' he added the proviso, 'if you're coming laddie, it wouldn't be wise to be bringing Meg. There's one or two of the laird's party don't seem to know what they are shooting at – one of them has already shot Annie MacDonald's cow – so it would be safest to leave the dog at home.' The boy was torn between wanting to go and yet not wanting to leave Meg behind.

'You'll go, of course,' his father advised.

'I'm not keen to leave Meg behind,' he objected.

'I will take good care of Meg,' his father promised.

The Woman nodded confirmation. 'I also will take care of her,' she said. But he ignored her.

When he returned he rather hoped his father would have brought Meg to the bus to meet him, and finding him not there he was disappointed but in no way apprehensive. When his father made a promise only death could have prevented him from keeping it.

As soon as he was in sight of the cottage he gave his special whistle which invariably brought Meg bounding towards him and when, after he repeated the whistle two or three times she had neither appeared nor even responded with a bark, he felt the needling of a premonition that something might be wrong. He hurried to the cottage and pushed open the door.

'Where's Meg?' he demanded abruptly.

Instantly he saw from the Woman's agitated expression that she had worrying news for him. 'Your father's out on the hill looking for her at this moment,' she confessed nervously. 'See it was like this . . .' The boy turned to go, not interested in hearing her explanation. All he needed to know was that Meg had somehow escaped his father's vigilance and had gone off on her own. She must be found as quickly as possible. 'You must listen to me, please,' the Woman begged. 'For your father's sake.'

Her plea did not stay him but the mention of his father made him pause, still fretting with impatience to begin the search. 'While you were from home old Peter McRae passed on and was buried just this morning. Naturally your father was needed to help carry the bier but before he left he made sure that Meg was safely closed in the byre and he'd padlocked it so it couldn't be opened accidentally. Well, while he was away the schoolmistress was here for a strupak and seeing Meg was safely shut away she let her own little beast go free. When she was ready to go there was no sign of it anywhere and she started to worry if it was up to mischief. I went out to help her look for it and all the time I was thinking how glad I was Meg was safely in the byre. It wasn't until I'd left her and was coming home that I saw the tunnelling that had been going on under the door of the byre. When I opened the door there was no sign, neither of Meg nor the schoolmistress's little beast.'

The kettle boiled over at that moment, spitting on to the glowing peats and demanding her attention.

'I'm away,' he shouted churlishly.

'But there's more I have to tell you,' she called, running after him. As the boy glowered at her he saw the wetness round her eyes and knew she'd been crying. But her tears did not move him.

'What more?' he demanded truculently.

'When the men were on their way home from the funeral they heard the barking of dogs, and the bleating of sheep from up on the hills, so they rushed to get their guns and go out after them. When I told your father that Meg had escaped . . .' She covered her eyes with her apron.

An icy hand seemed to grip the boy's stomach and a great lump formed in his throat. Without a word he dashed off towards the hills, stopping every now and then to call and whistle Meg, but his calls and whistles seemed only to become absorbed in the silence. There was no bark of recognition and no dark shape apperared at his heels. And then, not far distant, there was the sound of a shot. The boy held his breath and stood so still that he might have been the target. Then there were two more shots followed by complete silence. He dared to raise his voice again and call Meg but it was his father who returned his call.

'You may as well come home now, laddie,' his father said. Dumbly the boy looked at him and as they walked side by side his father asked, 'You know what's been happening up there?' The boy nodded. 'The shepherd's shot one of them. That little beast of the schoolmistress's, I believe. Being white it was easy to get a shot at it. That's one that won't be worrying another sheep,' his father finished with grim satisfaction.

'What like was the other dog?' the boy asked in a strained voice. His father did not answer immediately. 'Meg is missing,' the boy added hoarsely.

'Was Meg not home when you left?' his father asked then.

'No,' the boy replied.

'We'll need to wait and see when she does come home,' his father said impassively.

They had been back at the cottage for little more than a quarter of an hour before they heard Meg scratching at the door. The boy half rose but it was the Woman who opened the door and, aghast at the dog's appearance, turned to look despairingly at her husband and then at the boy. The rank smell of sheep fleece commingled with the putrid smell of stale blood filled the kitchen as Meg, panting heavily, padded over to the boy and dropped at his feet. But neither by word nor by gesture did he acknowledge her presence. He had seen all he needed to see: the slavering jaws; the wisps of fleece still clinging to her teeth; the snout and the heart-shaped white patch red and sticky with blood all proclaimed her guilt and, slumped back in his chair, he knew beyond all doubt that there could be no reprieve for her.

When the shepherd arrived, still flushed and angry after his exertions he said, 'Aye, folks were saying it was her but by God! She'll never get the chance to kill again. Seventeen sheep they've killed or maimed between them. Seventeen! And that's only what we've found so far. I took a couple of shots at her there but she was too wily.' He glared at the boy. 'First thing in the morning she's got to be put down.' The shepherd had given his ultimatum.

'That will surely be done,' his father affirmed quietly and then gave the shepherd a dram of whisky to soothe him. In a mellower tone the shepherd admitted, 'I'd never have thought the day would come when I'd have to have your dog shot, laddie. The way she was attached to you I'd never have believed she'd have been tempted to go off on her own.'

His father explained how it had happened.

'Aye,' the shepherd agreed, 'I knew I'd have to shoot that little beast one day. Those terrier dogs are a menace in sheep country. They shouldn't be allowed. The pity of it is they can sometimes get another dog excited enough to go with them and then once they get the sheep on the run and a taste of blood they're like a pack of wolves. There's no other way but to shoot them.'

The boy remained miserably silent, knowing it would be

133

futile to beg mercy for his dog. The maxim 'once a sheep killer always a sheep killer' had been instilled into him ever since he was old enough to recognize a sheep.

'You could get the Cruelty to do it for you,' the shepherd suggested. The boy's recoil was instant. He'd once witnessed the Cruelty inspector trying to dispose of an ailing cow. It had taken four attempts! He could still remember the nausea he'd felt then. 'Or I'll take her back with me tonight and get rid of her,' the shepherd offered, intending to be kind.

'No!' The boy couldn't be sure if it was himself or his father who uttered the word so vehemently.

As the shepherd was taking his leave he said, 'I'll tell you what, laddie, I'll give you a pup from the next litter my best bitch has. It'll be a good one.'

The boy's lips tightened. It was the only indication he gave that he was conscious of the offer. His father murmured a dismissive acknowledgement.

Once the shepherd had gone the Woman tactfully went to bed. He and his father sat for some time before there was any word spoken between them.

'It's bad, laddie, but there's nothing to be done about it. You know that?' The boy's wide tragic eyes were fixed on his father as he nodded his head in assent. 'It will please me if you will try not to blame Molly for any of this,' his father said, a hint of pleading in his voice. 'It was no fault of hers that Meg got out and did what she did.' Again it was only the boy's tightened lips that betrayed his feelings. 'Molly's fairly upset about it, I can tell you, laddie. I believe she would have given a lot not to have this happen to you,' his father appealed. 'She's mighty fond of you, laddie.' Perceiving no reaction from his son he stood up, saying he too was going to bed. As he passed by the boy he laid a comforting hand on his shoulder. 'You stay in your bed for a whiley in the morning,' he advised gently. 'I'll take her away. You won't need to hear anything.'

The boy faced his father steadily. 'No!' he insisted in a clipped, flat tone. 'I will do it myself.' He watched his father go to the closet where his gun was kept; watched as he placed two cartridges on the table. And almost as soon as the sky had dimmed, dawn began to reassert itself . . .

After he'd replaced and trodden down the last sod on the grave the boy looked with loathing at his gun, still lying on the ground where he'd left it. For some minutes he stood there as if mesmerized by the sight of it until with sudden resolve he seized it and went running and leaping down the hill until he reached the burn. There, raising the gun in a manner that verged on the sacrificial, he brought the barrel down heavily on the nearest boulder. Again and again he brought it down until, satisfied at last, he hurled the distorted remains into the rushing, tumbling burn. His stiff shoulders sagged as he watched the swift-flowing water seize and impel the gun over and over between the rocks, onward and downward towards the sea.

As he climbed upwards to gain one of the winding and criss-crossed sheep tracks which led in the direction of the crofts, the drifting mist thinned enough to reveal a shawled figure standing motionlessly on a hillock which overlooked the glen. The figure looked as if it had been standing there for some time. She'd been spying on him! She, the Woman had come out deliberately to spy on him. She, the Woman, for he knew instinctively that it was she, had followed and spied on him! What right had she to be there? Fury goaded him on but, determined to ignore her, he dropped to a lower path. She moved down the hill as if to waylay him

As their paths met he tried to sidestep her but she reached out and caught his arm. 'Laddie!' she begged in a low, urgent voice.

'I have nothing I want to say to you,' he rebuffed her, trying to shrug off her restraining hand.

'Laddie! Please.' She clung to him and the timbre of her voice made him pause. But he would not look at her. 'Laddie, cannot you see I'm grieving for you? Surely my own heart's that sore that such a thing should have to happen.'

Relentlessly he cut her short. 'It didn't have to happen, did it? It was mainly your fault that it happened.' It gave him a degree of satisfaction to see her wince.

'I'm not denying I'm a lot to blame but I was never wise to the ways of terrier dogs. It never came into my mind that it would dig its way into the byre and that Meg would be lured out by it.' His young mouth twisted cynically but she persisted, 'Oh, if only you wouldn't hate me so much, laddie. And for what cause? I've never expected you to put me in place of your mother any more than your father would want it. Oh, I know your father doesn't think so much of me as he did of your mother, and he never will do but he's kind and good to me and I've only ever expected to help ease his loss a little. Just as I've wanted to help you, laddie. And now I've given you cause to hate me and I shudder at my own ignorance that's been responsible for it.' She paused and looked out to where the sea was hidden by mist. He flicked a look at her and saw that her eyes were brimming with tears.

'I've suffered loss too, laddie. A loss I know I'll never recover from.' Her hand slid from his arm but he made no move to go. 'I once had to kill something I loved. It was a long time back when I was no more than seventeen years old but the memory of it will haunt me for the rest of my life.' She drew a long, uneasy breath. He looked up at her slowly and seeing she had captured his interest she went on. 'I had a babe in my belly but because there was no man to marry me and my father was so strict and so proud of his position in the church I couldn't give it life. The disgrace of having a daughter who was pregnant and no man willing to marry her would have near killed my father and I daresay my mother with him so I made an excuse to go off to Glasgow and I hardened my heart and went to one of the places where they attend to these things.' She gave a deep broken sigh. 'The guilt of it will never leave me,' she whispered. She glanced at him and he caught her strained expression. 'I don't know what's come over me that I should be telling you of such things but when I married your father I prayed I'd be able to share in the feeling you and he have for each other. Just a wee left-over would have contented me but I see little chance of that now.'

The boy kicked peevishly at a tough clump of heather.

'Ach,' he conceded gruffly, 'I daresay it wasn't so much your fault.'

With a sudden gesture she raised her hands and held his flushed cheeks, compelling him to look at her. 'If only we could both bring ourselves to believe that, perhaps we might be able to share our sorrow, and shared sorrow would surely lead to a lessening of your dislike of me, laddie. How much happier our home would be for the three of us, surely?'

Indignant and embarrassed he pulled her hands away from his face. 'I don't dislike you all that much,' he mumbled, and in a moment of surprise recognized it might be the truth.

He saw her chin lift fractionally. 'Your father will be wondering where the two of us have got to,' she said. 'He'll be out of his bed by now.' Turning she began hurrying back towards the crofts while the boy, still lacerated by the torment of the last twelve hours, dawdled some distance behind her, not wanting to get back much before the time he would have to leave for school.

It would not do to dodge school just because of what had happened, he told himself. It would be there that he would have to face his next trial of strength over his ability to conceal his feelings. It would be there he would best learn to maintain his mask of impassivity when they spoke of Meg; there that his schoolmates would crowd about him, not primarily to offer sympathy but to compliment him on his courageous decision to carry out the deed himself and on his skilful accomplishment of it.

As he expected, the day proved to be one of torture, every thoughtless exchange inflicting a fresh wound. But he had not weakened under their clamour for details. He had not disgraced his Highland upbringing.

The day had turned stormy and as soon as lessons were over his friends, with only a brief grumble at the weather, ran off to their homes leaving him hunched dejectedly in the shelter of the playground wall. With no Meg racing to meet him the rest of the evening loomed desolately and for the first time in his life he would have welcomed a good pile of homework rather than the copying of an easy map which would take less than half an hour. He stretched out the time it normally took him to reach the cottage by seeking shelter from the storm behind convenient rocks but as the sky darkened prematurely and sharp hailstones began to sting his face he submitted to their onslaught and, head down, made his way homewards.

His father was packing shingle under the door of the byre and, going to him, the boy handed back the second cartridge. A nod of complete understanding passed between them.

In the kitchen the Woman was standing beside the table straining crowdie into a basin. She smiled at him tentatively but, suspicious that her smile might have a weakening effect on him, he ignored her and went into his bedroom where he threw himself down on to his bed, numbed and exhausted by the events of the day. He heard his father's voice as he came into the kitchen and knew it would soon be time for their evening meal. As the appetizing smell of the Woman's cooking seeped under the door he wondered if she had succeeded in easing the burden of his father's unhappiness? Whether she would ever succeed in easing his? He doubted it. He could not imagine ever forgiving her for Meg. Not ever. Not ever, his mind repeated.

But that night, as hovering sleep relaxed his body and blurred the harsh images in his mind, a strange new idea filtered into his consciousness. 'Maybe sometime,' it seemed to suggest. 'Sometime.' And when he wakened next morning he was surprised to find the new idea less strange.

8

The Little Warrior

The small white motor boat rounding the sgurr of rock at the entrance to the bay caught Martha McKinnon's eye as she was on her way to fill a creel of peats from the stack at the end of the cottage. All morning, wherever she'd been working she had been watching out for such a sight and now, stopping in her tracks, she put down her empty creel and stood with her arms folded across her chest, her inscrutable gaze fixed upon the boat as it speared into the bay. After a few minutes she could make out that the solitary figure at the tiller had begun to wave expansively and with a stiff uplifted arm, she responded to the greeting.

As the boat neared the shore she drew in a deep breath of satisfaction. My son, she reflected proudly. My son whom I alone have nurtured from birth to near manhood with the help of neither mate nor master. And now this day has come. This day that I have worked and planned for. This day when I stand here in front of my own house to witness my son come home at the helm of his own boat. Herself descended from generations of island fishermen, she had an ancestral conviction that a man born within sight and sound of the sea must aspire, above all else, to be in charge of his own boat. Both she and her son had accepted, almost from his childhood, that such must be the objective for which they both would strive, and at last, due mainly to her determination, their target had been reached before his seventeenth birthday.

All they must wait for now was the top of the tide when the men from the village would be coming to haul the boat up the shore to the safety of its winter berth. Under her tight-folded arms her flat chest swelled and there was a semblance of regality about her raised chin as the boat's engine was throttled down and a mooring splashed into the water.

It had been a grim struggle to save enough to buy the boat. The croft she had inherited from her father had provided them with a sufficiency of good plain food, warm clothing and peats for fuel, but isolated as it was there had been only limited opportunities for either herself or her son to earn a cash reward for their labours. Summer campers had bought eggs and milk; there were the occasional bed and breakfasts wanted by climbers; the chance lobster caught by her son and sold to eager holidaymakers and the rare hiring out of her father's heavy old dinghy to amateur fishermen keen to try their skill.

In earlier days she had been an adept knitter and had sold much of her work to shops on the mainland but the payment had been meagre and now she found it more profitable to put aside her knitting during the winter months and join the winkle gatherers who, for the four hours between tides, went scrabbling among the boulders and shingle of the shore. But it was mercilessly hard work. After stumbling and slithering hazardously from boulder to boulder she had to crouch in icy pools with the sea washing her long skirts while with bare hands she clawed among the seaweed and wet shingle to find the clusters of tiny shellfish. Exposed to every kind of weather – gale-force winds which despite her sturdy frame frequently managed to unbalance her; lashing rain; bullet-like hail; blinding snow showers and stinging spray – she laboured to fill pail after pail of winkles which were then tipped into hundredweight sacks – eight pails to the sack – and roped to her back to be carried up the steep half mile of brae where the lorry driver collected them. But the work paid better than knitting and the return was quicker so, subjugating her discomfort to the achievement of her goal, she had pressed on indefatigably.

Between the work on the croft and the winkle gathering there had been no respite, but as the weight of coins in the old tea caddy had increased and the tied bundle of notes had thickened so had her resolve strengthened and though she had cause to regret that the unrelenting toil had coarsened her fingers to such tree-bark roughness that her knitting was now confined to heavy socks and stockings, she neither noticed nor cared that at forty-five years old she could have been taken for twenty years older.

'Are you hearing me, Mother?' Her son's voice hailed her from the boat. 'I'm wanting the dinghy if I'm to get ashore!'

'Coming, Alistair!' she called and dragging the small lightweight dinghy into the water she rowed the fifty yards or so to where the boat was swinging at the mooring.

'So you're back!' Her voice had such a slight intonation of welcome that a stranger might have described it as being indifferent.

Alistair was not deceived by her tone. 'Aye, I'm back,' he agreed, equally expressionlessly. 'Are you coming aboard?' He gave her a hand to help her over the side.

As he was tying the painter of the dinghy she asked, 'And are you well pleased with the boat now you have her?'

'I reckon so. She's a pretty good bargain for the money, I'm thinking,' he admitted. He lifted the floorboard, frowned a little and then began to work the pump.

'She's sound?' his mother was quick to inquire, though her voice betrayed only a fraction of the concern which had been lodged in her mind since three days previously when he had set off alone to bring the boat from the mainland harbour.

'Aye, she's sound enough. She took in a fair bit of water when she was first launched but she'd been lying for a whiley so it was only to be expected. She soon took up again. I daresay she'll be the better of a good caulking but as soon as she's hauled up there'll be time enough for that.'

His mother's glance ranged over the boat, approving the height of the bow, the breadth of the beam, the sheerline and the appearance of the timbers before it came to rest on her son as he bent over the engine. She could not bring herself to display her feelings but she was overjoyed that he was safely back home and the glint in her eyes revealed her joy to him when he looked up unexpectedly and caught her off guard. His lips flexed a little.

'You were lucky the calm weather held until you got back,' she remarked.

'Indeed don't I know it,' he agreed. 'All the same I wouldn't have been bothered by a bit of a blow. I'd know better then how she'd be likely to take it. It would have been a good test for her.'

'That will likely come soon enough,' she predicted, looking up at the sky. 'I'd be best pleased if I could see some sign of the men coming,' she added uneasily.

'Ach, there's time enough yet,' he assured her. 'And the bay's calm enough.'

'And for how much longer?' she demanded. Her mouth tightened. Habituated all her life to wild weather, she mistrusted calm spells. They were good while they lasted but that was never for more than a day or two. And whereas you were always prepared for gales, calm caught you unawares and just as you were permitting yourself to make the most of it, it would be bullied away within minutes by a gale that seemed all the fiercer after the lull.

There was no safe winter anchorage in the bay and before Alistair had been able to arrange his trip to the mainland to collect the boat and bring it back to the island they had needed to wait until the prospect of a brief spell of calm weather had coincided with one of the bi-monthly peak tides necessary to get it out of the water and well out of reach of the winter storms. There had been weeks, even months of frustration but now as soon as help arrived the worry and suspense would be over. The boat would be hauled up the narrow inlet already cleared among the boulders, man-handled over the shingle and laid snugly in the shelter of the cottage where it would stay until the spring brought more settled weather. It would then be re-launched ready for Alistair to begin lobster fishing with the creels he intended to make during the winter months.

'Well,' Alistair interrupted her thoughts. 'What d'you think of her yourself now you've had a good look at her?' He eyed her keenly.

'She's fine,' she conceded and he knew that, coming from her, the remark could be construed as enthusiasm. 'I didn't see a name on her,' she pointed out. 'Does she not have a name?'

'Ach, she had some fancy name like Loongana or Lugano. Something like that. It wasn't right for a boat at all so I painted it out before I started.' He paused for a moment. 'I was thinking I might call her *Martha*,' he suggested teasingly.

'You will do nothing of the kind,' she derided. '*Martha* is as foolish a name for a boat as the one you spoke of.'

'Martha was faithful,' he reminded her.

'Indeed but if you're going by the good book then don't be looking for a name to call her by. Your boat has a motor and so needs none of the Lord's breath to sail her.'

He shrugged. It was much the reaction he'd expected and when his mother said no it was useless to try to persuade her otherwise. Anyway, he himself wasn't too keen on naming the boat *Martha*. He'd thought only to please her.

She said, 'If you'll row me ashore I'll put on the potatoes. You'll need to get some food into you before you begin the job of pulling the boat up.'

'Indeed I will so, but wait now a minute.' Turning he retrieved a parcel from the cuddy. 'The old man I got the boat from gave me these kippers,' he explained, handing her the parcel. 'I'm fancying a couple or so with my potatoes.'

'And no doubt the men will be fancying the same when they smell them,' she declared. 'I'll have them ready for when they've done hauling.'

While he was taking her back to the shore she scanned the tide line. 'To my way of thinking it will be two hours maybe before the tide is at its height.'

'Aye, I reckon about that,' Alistair agreed. 'We should manage to have her up before it's dark. Mind you,' he added, 'there'll be a moon likely.'

His mother surveyed the horizon calculatingly. 'I'm not so sure of it,' she said. Her eyes lifted to the hill, tracing the meandering dark stain which marked the path along which the men would be coming.

Ashore she set about preparing a meal and by the time she heard his footsteps on the cobbles the food was ready to be put on his plate. 'How's the tide?' she asked him.

'It's coming in fairly quick,' he told her. 'I'm thinking there must be a good bit more breeze outside the bay.'

'And are there yet no signs of the men coming?'

'Not a one,' he replied fretfully. 'And seeing that's the way of it I doubt they'll be here in time.'

'Not be here in time?' Her voice was sharp-edged. 'Why not indeed? What would be keeping them back when they promised that they would come?'

'They promised they would come the minute they knew they were needed,' Alistair corrected her. 'But it's likely they wouldn't know it was today that it would be. It was not until first light this morning that I could be sure myself that it was calm enough for me to set out. I couldn't get word to them at that hour.'

'Could you not have called in at Drinen and told them they were needed? They would have had plenty of time still.'

'I did just that but there wasn't a man to be seen there. The Red Widow was down on the shore getting seaweed and she told me the men were all away to the cliffs over at Slochan. Bheinn Ruari's cow had fallen into the big yaw there and they'd taken ropes and slings to try would they get her out.'

'But did you not leave a message with her to tell the teacher to send one of the schoolchildren to say the men were needed for tonight's tide?'

'Surely I did but they have that Sassenach schoolteacher there while Morag is in hospital and it's likely she wouldn't think it important enough to send one of the scholars. Anyway,' he went on, 'the Red Widow was saying I had no need to worry about getting the boat ashore tonight because she'd been up at the post office listening to the wireless and she'd heard them saying the weather would be staying calm for the next day or two.'

'The Red Widow!' exclaimed his mother scornfully. 'With what little sense the Red Widow has in her head she might just as easily have been hearing the forecast for Timbuctoo.'

'Aye,' he admitted, 'I wouldn't have thought much about

144

what she said hadn't the old man that had the boat told me the same thing before I set out this morning. Gales only in Iceland according to the wireless, he said.'

'Wireless!' His mother's mouth twisted cynically. 'Ach, those fools! They don't warn you of a gale coming until it's hit you and there's no doubt of it. I trust my own eyes and the feeling in my bones to acquaint me with the weather more so than any old wireless.'

She went to the door and looked anxiously over the bay to where the evening sun was dipping to meet its reflection in the water. She carried on to the edge of the incoming tide and, detecting the hissing menace in the mounting surge, her anxiety increased. The forecasters could not delude her about it staying calm, she complained fiercely to herself. There was undeniably wind on the way and her only doubt was about its force.

When she returned to the cottage she found Alistair peering at the hill with the aid of his grandfather's old telescope. 'No sign of anyone?' she asked.

'None,' he confirmed shortly.

'What has come over them that they would save a cow before a boat?' she demanded scathingly but Alistair neither looked at her nor replied.

'Surely some of them will come in time,' she went on.

'You think we're in for a good blow then?' he asked, knowing she had a far better eye for the weather than he himself.

'I have no doubt of it,' she told him.

He wandered down to inspect the cleared inlet and when he came back he looked even more concerned. 'If they would get here within the half hour we'd still manage it,' he said, but the expression on his mother's face told him that in her judgement it was already too late.

Adding weight to her prediction of a change in the weather the cows came home earlier that evening and were already waiting outside the byre to get at the hay they would be expecting to find in the mangers. She urged them in, fed them and then hastened to get the pail and begin milking. When she had finished she hurried to the house to sieve the milk and pour it into the setting bowls and then she made haste to collect the eggs and close up the hens. She knew her hurrying was for no particular purpose; that it was her own need to have her mind free to agonize over her son's dilemma that was driving her so relentlessly.

As she passed Alistair's work shed on the way back to the cottage he emerged carrying an anchor over his shoulder. Disillusionment slowed her pace. 'They'll not get here in time now,' he told her. 'There's nothing for it but to put out another anchor and hope the wind won't get too strong, or if it does, that it won't shift to the north-west.'

She almost winced. The bay was totally unsheltered from the north-west. Pensively she watched him rowing out to the launch and not until she'd heard the splash of the anchor did she go indoors. Putting more peats on the fire, she hooked the kettle over it and then lit the lamp before divesting herself of her homespun jacket and the old black beret which, ever since it had been left behind by one of the bed and breakfasters some years previously, had been her regular outdoor headwear. Putting on an apron to signify that her outside work was finished and she was now changed for the evening, she sat down and took up her knitting but she was unable to settle.

After all their years of saving and struggling to get the boat and after all the patient waiting and the planning to have it safely ashore before the winter storms, being thwarted on the very eve of their achievement not by the elements but by the casualness of those on whom they had so confidently relied had shattered her, fragmenting the happiness she had experienced when she had first seen the boat entering the bay.

Her prediction of rough weather became a certainty and her mind became a turmoil of questioning. How quickly would the wind rise? How strong and from which direction? How long would it blow? Would the little boat be able to ride it? Would the anchor drag? She composed herself as a figure passed the window. Alistair came in, his hair tousled by the wind.

'It's fairly blowing up outside the bay,' he announced.

146

Determined not to add to his apprehension she said, 'Maybe it's quick come, quick die.'

'I hope so,' he said. 'It's quick enough coming anyway,' and hardly had he finished speaking before the gale was announcing its approach, tentatively at first with random buffetings at the roof and then with increasingly full-throated roars in the chimney. Alistair moved restlessly about the kitchen while his mother strove to give the impression she was concerned only with her knitting, and though they rarely exchanged any comments on the weather, each was aware that the other was listening intently to the rising wind and observing the deepening darkness of the moonless sky. From time to time Alistair went to stand outside the door and on each occasion, when he came inside again, his mother looked at him question-ingly though she never voiced the question. At last he volunteered with studied indifference, 'She seems to be riding it out well enough so far, from what I can make out.'

'Did you not say yourself she's a good sea boat?' his mother countered with as much reassurance as she could muster.

It was not until around midnight that they had heard the sound that they had been waiting and yet dreading to hear – the thumping of the wind against the door and the peppering of flung spray on the window. They looked at each other steadily.

'That's it!' Alistair's voice was harsh with consternation. His mother nodded sombre agreement. The wind had shifted to the north-west.

'Maybe it will keep on shifting yet,' she suggested, though she had only a forlorn hope that it might do so.

'Not before it's done damage it won't, I reckon,' Alistair said bitterly. 'And I doubt it will drop before the morning tide now.'

His mother stifled a pious sigh. 'It must be as the Lord wills,' she murmured.

While the wind worked itself up into a full gale they sat in the kitchen, neither of them having any thought of going to their beds, both of them attempting to find solace for their stretched nerves by drinking innumerable mugs of tea. In silence they shared each other's alarm. Listening, they were fearful of what they might hear. Thinking, they feared their thoughts, and constantly, the image of a little boat battling against the storm occupied their minds.

At one juncture Alistair rose and, pulling on his oilskins, made for the door. As he opened it the kitchen was filled with the noise and wildness of the night.

'Alistair! What are you about?' his mother recalled him sharply.

'I'm wanting just to see will I get out to her,' he replied.

'You're mad to think of it!' she expostulated. 'No man in his senses would try to put out a dinghy on a night like this. You'll be drowned surely!'

Paying no heed to her he closed the door behind him and, panic-stricken by his words, she paused only to put on her jacket and beret before she followed him, pushing breathlessly against the charging wind to make her way to the dinghy. Hardened as she was to stormy weather, tonight the crashing breakers sounded more vengeful; the surging swell more voracious; the noise of boulders being sucked back by the receding tide more like the angry grinding of some monster's teeth than she had ever before encountered. If Alistair was determined to contend with such a sea she was certain she would soon have no son. She imagined the sea greedily engulfing him and taking him far beyond any help. She imagined his body being hurled against the cruel rocks. Somehow she must prevail upon him not to take such a risk and though she had never previously permitted herself to unbend sufficiently to beg him to accede to a plea of hers she was so disabled by fear that she knew she must do it now.

He already had the dinghy near the edge of the tide. She grasped the gunwale and leaned towards him. 'Alistair,' she entreated urgently, but at that moment a breaker, its black menace white-crested in the darkness, rolled towards them and, breaking over the dinghy, swirled her off her feet. Losing her grip on the dinghy she fell heavily, and as she tried to get to her knees the next breaker surged over her. She heard Alistair's voice calling to her.

'I'm all right,' she gasped, staggering out of the water. 'But you've no chance of getting any dinghy into that sea this night.'

'No,' he said angrily, and seizing the gunwale he tipped out the water and turned the boat in preparation for them to drag it up the shore.

The lamplit window of the cottage seemed doubly inviting as, shaken and bedraggled, they picked their way towards it. Immediately she put the kettle on the hook.

'I'm away to my bed,' Alistair announced. And then, with his hand on the latch of his bedroom door he said, 'It wouldn't have been right for me not to try to get to her.' They exchanged a brief glance of understanding.

'You'll not be waiting for a strupak?' she asked but he had already closed the door of his bedroom.

While the ketttle boiled she towelled and tidied her hair and then, draping her wct clothes over the back of a chair, she set the chair beside the fire. Wrapping herself in a blanket she went to lie on the recess bed, leaving the curtains undrawn for fear Alistair should attempt to reach the boat.

Despite her tiredness she had no desire to sleep and as she lay, tight-lipped and dry-eyed, she could too easily detect the frequent sounds of restless creakings as her son tossed and turned and rose from his bed and lay down again. She too wanted to rise and strain to see if there was yet enough light for the boat to be visible but Alistair's ears would be as alert as her own. He would be bound to hear her, and knowing how much she was worrying would only add to his own torment. She was certain he would be as far from sleep as she was herself and her heart ached for him. The loss of the boat would be a severe enough blow for her. For him the agony of it would pierce even deeper. She wanted to pray but her mind was too bleak to marshal the form of her prayers. 'The Dear Lord save us,' she could only beseech inadequately and repetitively. The night seemed interminable and though she willed herself to lie quietly she cringed every time a breaker seemed to crash more thunderously. Rigidly controlling her tight-strung nerves she listened, as she knew her son must be listening, but to what were their ears attuned other than the roar of the sea? Was it for the first perceptible sign of the storm abating? Or was it for another sound entirely – the death throes of a boat being dashed to splinters on the rocks?

With a faint thinning of the darkness over the horizon there came an awareness that the wind had again shifted direction and now it was accompanied by the pounding of heavy rain on the roof. She rose quickly. Rain dampened down the sea, she reasoned, and with a shift in the wind direction if the boat was still afloat it might stand a chance yet. She dressed in her partly dried clothes and knocked on Alistair's door. As she expected he was standing by the window, his hands in his pockets, his shoulders slumped dejectedly.

'Can you make her out yet?' She hated having to put the question, the answer to which could desolate them both.

'Aye,' he said and in the single syllable there was pathos almost beyond bearing.

'What's wrong?' she demanded.

'See for yourself,' he bade her, and moved aside. After moments of intense peering she managed to make out the faint outline of the boat.

'See what's happened?' he asked distractedly. 'The burn's in spate and it's pushing her beam on to the sea. She's taking them green now. There's no doubt she's a splendid sea boat or she wouldn't have lasted the night but now this will be the end of her.' His voice broke and then took on a testy note. 'I'd sooner she'd gone in the night when I couldn't see her rather than have to watch her go down. It would have been easier to bear.'

A beaten expression settled on his mother's face. If he loses the boat he'll no longer wish to stay in this place, she thought. He'll be wanting to go somewhere that's more kindly to boats and to men. Somewhere he'll have more chance to earn and save money. He'll have no heart for this kind of struggle again. I shall have to stay here alone. The surmise plagued her and yet, mindful of how incomplete life would seem to him without a boat, she accepted that she must make no attempt to dissuade him. Aloud she said, 'There could be a lull when the tide changes.'

His only response was a despairing shrug of his shoulders. For a moment she longed to embrace him but the abiding fear of making him less of a man had for so long forced her to quell such instincts that she knew it was too late now. He would instantly suspect she had gone out of her mind. Compassion for him overwhelmed her own anguish, and unable to offer comfort she returned to the kitchen where she began preparing their breakfast porridge, insensible of the fact that the rhythm of stirring the meal into the water was according with the rhythm of her silent invocations to her God. When the porridge was ready she half filled a bowl from the pan, put a knob of butter into the centre and then called her son. He came listlessly, filled up his bowl with milk and went to stand by the window.

After a little while he said, 'I believe you yourself might be able to make her out now.' She glanced at him and rose quickly, puzzled by the dullness of his tone. Joining him by the window, she stared fixedly at the dawn-streaked darkness until eventually she could clearly discern the boat wallowing beam on to the rolling breakers. There was little joy in the sight. Though the boat was still afloat the sluggishness of its response to the seas was telling its own tale. Despite its gallant resistance, as each wave broke it settled lower and lower in the water until it was only too evident it was drastically close to foundering. Every now and then the bow of the boat managed to lift feebly as if imploring help. Martha's desire to save it, even at this last minute, grew so intense her body felt as if it would burst with exaggeration of its own power and a recklessness of resolve she was aware she could never sustain. And yet there was nothing either she or Alistair could do save watch in impotent anger and sadness until the boat disappeared beneath the waves.

The light was growing steadily, emphasizing the plight of the boat. Alistair went outside and she saw him going past the window on the way to his shed. She sought for threads

151

of hope. The swell was pounding at the shore but the tide must be close to low, if it wasn't low already. If the men would come they would be able to launch the heavy dinghy and perhaps get out to the boat. If the wind would shift just enough to shelter the part of the bay from which she and Alistair could launch the small dinghy there might still be a chance. As she poured hot water into the bowl ready to wash the dishes her hands seemed nerveless with despair. The door opened and Alistair burst into the kitchen.

'I'm thinking I've a good chance of getting out to her now. Come and give me a push with the dinghy, will you?'

'Surely there's too much swell yet,' she argued but he cut her short.

'If you'll not help me then I'll do it myself,' he retorted and strode out of the house.

She went after him. He's crazy, she told herself. He'll see that well enough when he tries. But he didn't see it and had the dinghy ready to launch by the time she reached it.

'Just give the stern a good push, as hard as you can as soon as I tell you,' he instructed. 'And then get well out of the way.'

'I'll come with you,' she said. 'With two of us to pull we might do it.' At the back of her mind was the thought that if he were to drown she would be with him.

'No!' His voice was vehement. 'I'll have the tide to help me now. I can row across it.'

When he commanded she pushed with all the strength she had left in her body and as the bow rose to meet the breaker she saw him pull mightily on the oars. The dinghy was afloat! But would the swell hurl it back? Her breath was tight in her chest as she watched it mount the first breaker and then the next and the next. She saw the prodigious effort her son was making and willed more strength into him. He was going to succeed.

As he pulled closer to the boat a rain squall swept across the bay, blotting out her view of what was happening, and when it cleared she could see he had reached the boat and was trying repeatedly to manoeuvre the dinghy so he could tie up. When at last he accomplished it a small sigh of relief escaped her. But she was still in the grip of her fear for him. He still had the dangerous task of somehow getting from the dinghy into the boat. Would he manage it safely? A second and more prolonged squall obscured her view and she was in an agony of suspense until it passed. When she had blinked the rain and salt spray from her eyes she saw the dinghy swinging astern and her son standing beside the boat's pump. 'The Lord save us,' she whispered thankfully, though she was only a degree less sure of her son's safety. 'The Lord save us!'

For some time she was unable to detect any change in the way the boat was countering the continued onslaught of the sea but then she perceived a gradually increasing buoyancy in its response. Her heart seemed to be lifting and plunging in unison with the bow and her body was quivering with reaction. The boat could be saved but unless the men arrived before the tide had risen too far it would have to spend another night at the mercy of the weather. She would wait, she decided, only until Alistair was safely ashore again and then she herself would make haste over the hill to the village and tell them how urgently they were needed. And they would come. The wireless forecast had evidently misled them but they would not be deluded a second time. She was sure they would come.

'How long till the men will be needed?' she asked Alistair as soon as he was safely ashore.

'No more than a couple of hours if we're to get her up on the morning tide,' he told her.

She sensed an air of elation about him and, though understanding it, she felt the need to caution him.

'I will go at once,' she stated. 'It will not take me so long. This is only a lull in the storm. It will be blowing up again before the day is out.'

'You have no need to go for anyone,' he told her and when he saw she was about to argue he pointed towards the hill. 'Can you not see?' he chaffed her. Her eyes picked out the scurrying figures strung out along the path and the sight gave her a sudden release from fear.

'They will be wanting a good meal when they've

finished,' she said tonelessly and went into the house to begin preparations.

The boat was safely hauled to its winter quarters, the men had taken their meal, fortified themselves with a few drams of whisky and had returned to their homes. As Martha had predicted the storm was rising again to its full fury but now she was sitting beside the fire knitting serenely, her mind long immunized against worrying over any damage even the most violent storm could inflict on their well-tested homestead.

Alistair, who had stayed out in his shed making the most of the fading light to finish some task he had embarked upon, came into the kitchen.

'Well son, that's a good day's work done, is it not?' she greeted him.

'Indeed it is so,' he agreed. 'And did you hear the men praising her and saying what a good sea boat she is? A true little warrior they were saying she must be to have come through a night like last night.'

'And you've not yet got round to deciding on a name for her,' his mother chided him. 'I was only thinking during the night if she'd gone down without being named it would have been like a child dying un-named.'

'Well she has a name now,' he assured her. 'That's why I was wanting to finish this before light went. See that now?' Triumphantly he displayed a white board with black lettering.

Martha leaned forward to read it. '*Little Warrior,*' she spelled out.

'That's what the men called her and I don't believe I could better it,' he said, looking at the board with more pride than she could approve. 'What do you think yourself?'

She nodded primly. 'It's as good a name for her as any other,' she granted.